wuthering high

wuthering high

a bard academy novel

cara lockwood

POCKET BOOKS   MTV BOOKS

New York   London   Toronto   Sydney

POCKET BOOKS, a division of Simon & Schuster, Inc.
1230 Avenue of the Americas, New York, NY 10020

This book is a work of fiction. Names, characters, places, and
incidents are products of the author's imagination or are used
fictitiously. Any resemblance to actual events or locales or persons,
living or dead, is entirely coincidental.

Copyright © 2006 by Cara Lockwood

MTV Music Television and all related titles, logos, and
characters are trademarks of MTV Networks, a division of
Viacom International Inc.

All rights reserved, including the right to reproduce
this book or portions thereof in any form whatsoever.
For information address Pocket Books, 1230 Avenue
of the Americas, New York, NY 10020

ISBN-13: 978-1-4165-2475-5
ISBN-10:   1-4165-2475-4

This MTV Books/Pocket Books trade paperback edition July 2006

10 9 8 7 6 5 4 3 2 1

POCKET and colophon are registered trademarks of
Simon & Schuster, Inc.

Manufactured in the United States of America

For information regarding special discounts for bulk purchases,
please contact Simon & Schuster Special Sales at 1-800-456-6798
or business@simonandschuster.com.

For Ms. Miller, Mr. Logan, Prof. Barnard, and all English teachers everywhere

Acknowledgments

Special thanks to Kate Kinsella, for all of her advice and guidance! Many thanks to Julie Antrobus, for helping me with the elusive psychology of the teenage mind.

As always, thanks to Mom, Dad, and Matt. Thanks to my husband, Daren, for letting me bounce ideas off of him at two in the morning. A heartfelt thanks to my editor, Lauren, my agent, Deidre, and everyone at the Knight Agency.

And thanks to all my friends who are still teens at heart—Bethie, Shannon, Christina, Jane, Kate, Jordan, Stacey, Linda, and Kelly. Thanks, guys!

wuthering high

One

Okay, I confess.

I did, sort of, on purpose, steal Carmen's credit card (Carmen = stepmom, but I refuse to call her anything with "mom" in the title, as she's only twenty-four and can't take care of a pet goldfish, much less be any kind of mother figure). And I did, kind of, intentionally, charge up a thousand dollars' worth of push-up bras. But, technically, my dad said I could use Carmen's credit card for emergencies, and since my social life hinges on my ability to fill out a shirt, it *was* an emergency. I mean, if I was an SAT analogy, I'd be flat : board; boobs : me.

And yes, it's true that I did total my dad's new BMW convertible. Although "totaled" is a strong word for spilling Diet Coke in my lap and accidentally jumping the curb and running into a tree. I wouldn't have been driving at all (I only have my learner's permit) except that my little sister, Lindsay, called me on my mobile hysterical because she'd pissed off some two-hundred-pound girl bully and needed to be picked up from school since she'd been too scared to ride the bus. Mom couldn't get Lindsay because she was at her standing Botox appointment, and Carmen (Anti-Mom) couldn't be bothered, since she was too busy spending my college fund at Neiman Marcus.

And let's face it, I did Dad a favor. He looked ridiculous driving that cherry-red two-seater BMW. He's bald, for God's sake. He looked like every other pathetic midlife-crisis victim.

And, finally, I'll admit, it is true that I came home drunk the night before my PSAT exam, and overslept the test. This was entirely Tyler's fault (Tyler is a cute but disreputable quarterback of the junior varsity football team who I went with for a brief time before I came to my senses). He's been trying to get into my Paul Frank panties since the summer before freshman year, and he spiked my drink with Everclear in the hopes of robbing me of my virginity. I'd heard the bad rumors about Tyler, but chose to ignore them. I shouldn't have. BTW, he got what he deserved: a front seat full of Redbull and Everclear vomit. It's my hope that he'll be cleaning chunks out of the leather interior of his Toyota Forerunner for weeks. Since him, I've been on a guyatus (hiatus from guys).

So—given the mitigating circumstances—you'd think that I would be given a little slack. After all, I'm fifteen. Aren't I supposed to be making mistakes? Isn't that what the teen years are for? I can't be perfect all the time.

cara lockwood

So what do my parents do? They don't ground me. No. That would be me getting off too easy, Dad says. And even when I try to pit Mom against Dad (for the last five years since their divorce, I've gotten very, very good at this), it doesn't work. For the first time in my parents' lives, they actually agree on something.

They're going to send me to a school for juvenile delinquents.

Me! I've barely done anything wrong, and I'm going to be going to school with a bunch of drug-using degenerates. How did this happen? I think Mom has been watching too many episodes of *Ricki Lake,* where drill sergeants yell at pregnant teenagers.

It's ridiculous. Beyond ridiculous.

I am not a delinquent. I've had very bad luck, but I'm not bad. At least, not yet. Everyone knows that when good people go to prison they end up becoming bad while they're there. Either that, or they get stabbed with a homemade knife in the shower. I'm not that innocent. I've seen episodes of *Prison Break.*

Granted, I'm not going to prison.

I'm going to a place called Bard Academy in some Nowheresville Island off the coast of Maine. I don't care if that is where great lobsters come from. I don't want to live there. The brochure for Bard Academy says, and I quote, "a home for troubled and misguided teens set on its own private island, guarded by the Atlantic Ocean, and accessible only by ferry, where our students probe the classics in a solid academic tradition."

I am not troubled, nor misguided. If anyone needs to go to delinquent boarding school, it's my dad. He changes wives more often than he changes shoes. And don't get me started on Mom. She's a total basket case. She doesn't date. She doesn't even go out, so I'm not quite sure why she's obsessed with looking young, except that I fear she's holding on to some vague hope that Dad will take her back. Why she would want that, I have no idea.

So, I'm being exiled to some form of Alcatraz for juveniles in the Atlantic. This is what I get for saving my dad from getting a melanoma on his scalp and for coming to the rescue of my ungrateful sister. It's the last time I do a good deed.

"You hate me, don't you? You do. You hate me," Mom says, as she stands in my bedroom watching me pack. I'm taking my time folding my clothes because a) I don't want to go, and b) I want to wring the last bit of anxiety out of the moment for Mom's sake. If I draw this out, then she's liable to start feeling sadness and regret, and she might just decide I shouldn't go. At this point, breaking Mom might be my only chance of salvation.

I can tell that Mom is feeling guilty, even though she's just had a Botox injection, so the only expression she can convey with her numbed face is slight confusion. It's a little unnerving. Sort of like talking to a mannequin.

"I don't hate you," I say, trying to be calm and composed. I'm the adult here, after all, even if I am the one who's being sent off to a school one thousand miles away. I was the shoulder Mom cried on when Dad left her five years ago for his secretary. He's divorced and remarried since then, and Mom has been on maybe two dates. I love Mom, I do. But her neediness sometimes is a bit scary.

"It was your dad's idea," Mom pleads with me. Of course it's Dad's doing. Mom would never have had the guts to send me off, but Dad's a different story. He's been trying to disown me pretty much since I started talking and could talk back to him.

"Well, we both know Dad makes bad decisions. Why do you still let him boss you around?"

"I don't let him boss me," she says.

"You didn't even ask him if he'd pay for your Botox. You should. He gave you those worry lines."

Mom reflexively touches her face.

"You're right," she says.

I'm just about to reel Mom in, when we're interrupted by the appearance of my little sister, Lindsay. She's wearing a pair of jeans and her new purple push-up bra from Victoria's Secret.

Lindsay, age thirteen, is a 34B, which is a full cup size bigger than me, since I barely fill out an A cup. It's a bit embarrassing when your younger sister wears a bigger bra than you do. I'm not sure what my chest is waiting for, perhaps an engraved invitation. Apparently, my breasts are like diva pop stars and like to be fashionably late. When they arrive, I imagine they'll also come with a list of outrageous demands, like that they'll only tolerate blessed Kabbalah water, white Bentleys, and green M&M's.

To make matters worse, Lindsay spreads her arms wide and cries, "Tah-dah!," as if she just pulled her boobs out of a black magician's hat. Show off.

"My baby's first Victoria's Secret bra," Mom cries, turning her attention to Lindsay. "My baby is all grown up."

Although Mom's face doesn't change expression, I hear a slight crack in her voice, the telltale sign of an impending emotional breakdown.

Mom is going through the early stages of menopause and is extremely emotional these days. I recently caught her crying in front of a Cingular One ad. It's embarrassing.

"Lindsay, put some clothes on," I say. Seriously, sometimes I feel like the only responsible adult around here. What is Mom thinking? "Since when is it okay to parade around in your underwear?"

"Miranda—this is a revolutionary new bra," Lindsay informs me. "The patent is pending!"

"You don't even know what a patent is," I snap.

Lindsay sticks her tongue out at me. I glance down at Lindsay's jeans and notice the strap of a matching purple thong sticking out from her jeans.

"A thong!" I cry.

Mom didn't let me wear one of those until a month ago. And that was only after I wrote a two-page essay on the devastating effects of panty lines on my self-esteem. "She's too young to wear a thong!"

"You wear them all the time," Lindsay points out.

"I'm two years older. Mom? Really." I cross my arms to show my disapproval. Mom just wipes a tear from her eye and then tries to hug us both. I squirm away. With Premenopausal Mom, you never know when you're going to be blindsided with a hug. Last week, she wanted a hug in public in the middle of the cereal aisle at the grocery store. Thanks to my quick reflexes, I avoided PPDA (Parental Public Display of Affection), and Mom got an armful of Special K.

Lindsay, however, isn't as quick as I am, and she gets the full force of Mom's bear hug. I smirk at her, while she makes a face over Mom's shoulder. There are some benefits to being older. Better reflexes.

Besides, it's about time Lindsay took one for the team. She's benefited from all my hard lobbying efforts to house-train the 'rents. Case in point: my hunger strike to wear lip gloss in eighth grade, the protracted negotiations to let us watch the TBS version of *Sex and the City,* and now the thong essays. At this rate, Lindsay will never have to learn to do anything for herself, since I'm always doing all the work. She doesn't even have to work to have cleavage like I do. I need two rolls of Charmin's double ply to get the hint of cleavage. Lindsay just went to sleep one night and woke up the next morning as Pamela Anderson. Life is not fair.

Lindsay sticks her tongue out at me behind Mom's

back. I squint at her. She's gloating over the fact that she's ruined my last reprieve. She'll live to regret it. With me gone, there will be no one to blame when she does something bad, like breaking another of Mom's Staffordshire dogs. Besides, one week alone with hug-crazy Mom and Lindsay will be begging her to let me come home.

Since Lindsay ruins my chances of a night-before reprieve, I set Plan B into motion. Plan B involves me dredging out the waterworks on the car ride to the airport, which I know Mom won't be able to resist. I put some Visine in my purse for a quick-change act.

Plan B is thwarted, however, when Dad and Carmen (Secretary #2 who became Wife #3—my dad doesn't even bother to be creative with his adultery) show up the next morning in their new black Range Rover. With Dad alone I might have had a chance. But Carmen is immune to tears, and even so, I'd never cry in front of her. It would be like admitting defeat.

They emerge from the car arguing about whose fault it is that they're late. They've only been married two months and they're already fighting. I would be gloating, except for the fact that I'm about to be sent off to Siberia and no one seems to care. Mom is dry-eyed when she hugs me. Lindsay smiles and points down at her feet. She's wearing a pair of my Steve Maddens. She's going to stretch them out with her extra-wide Fred Flintstone feet.

"Stay out of my closet," I mouth to her as I duck into Dad's backseat. She just sticks out her tongue at me in defiance and then mouths, "Try and stop me," as Dad backs out of the driveway.

"Nice car," I say to Dad, meaning the opposite. The leather interior smells so strongly of new car, I feel a little nauseous. I can't believe Dad bought a Range Rover when just three months ago he told Mom he wanted to reduce his child-support payments. "I thought that *Consumer Reports* ranked Range Rovers as the car that breaks down the most."

I don't know if this is true, but I remember Tyler saying something about it. Back when I cared what he said, before he assaulted me.

Dad's eyes flick to mine in the rearview mirror. He frowns at me. "You're the reason I had to buy a new car in the first place."

I scoff. "How about a Honda? Mom has an Accord that's ten years old."

Dad turns a little red. He doesn't like it when I point out that we're poor. "Young lady, this is why you're on your way to Bard Academy," he says.

"Why? Because I tell you the truth?"

"I can't believe you let her talk to you like that," Carmen says, as if it's any of her business.

At the airport, Carmen stays in the car. She's still not talking to me because of the credit card incident. She says she hasn't lived down the embarrassment of having her credit card denied at Saks Fifth Avenue. Never mind that she charged ten thousand dollars' worth of purchases the month before, which meant that my one grand put the card over its maximum.

But, naturally, I'm the bad guy. I get it.

Dad, whose parenting skills have pretty much been limited to giving me lectures whenever I do something wrong, starts in on his "this hurts me more than it hurts you" lecture, the one he's been using since I was four and he'd sit me in the corner for time-outs. I can almost repeat it, word for word.

"Now, I know you think we're punishing you. But this is for your own good," Dad says as we're standing together inside the lobby of the airport. Carmen is outside in the car, pouting. Dad will probably have to buy her a few more thousand dollars' worth of Tiffany jewelry for him to be back in her good graces. Probably only a semester's worth of tuition or so.

"One day you'll realize that we're doing this because we care about you. This hurts us more than it hurts you."

This would be a moving speech, except that Dad is looking at his watch while he makes it. He's late for his tee time at the club. Honestly, I don't get any respect around here. This is my life we're talking about, and Dad is worried about getting to the putting green.

Dad is the opposite of Mom. Where Mom will blindside you with PPDA in the grocery store, Dad goes to great lengths to avoid PPDA in any context. The closest he'll get to actually hugging you is grabbing you in a side hug that he'll quickly turn into a headlock. As if he is saying, "I didn't mean to hug you—I want to wrestle," which is somehow less embarrassing, he thinks. I hate it, though. He always manages to mess up my hair.

He does this now, in fact. He puts his hand on my head and gives it a rough rub, like I'm a dog.

"You'll do great there, kiddo. I know you will," he says.

I walk toward the metal detectors and the security line. I turn around to see if Dad is still there, but he's already gone.

It's official. My life blows.

Two

The only time I've ever been away from home was the summer before fifth grade, right before my parents divorced. They shipped me and Lindsay off to some lame camp in Wisconsin where we were supposed to learn how to make keychains and canoe. I mean, I don't do the outdoors. My idea of roughing it is shopping at Active Endeavors.

Lindsay, because she's not right in the head, actually enjoyed the hikes, even though she got a nasty case of poison ivy. After that, she was stuck indoors and agreed with me that a camp lacking basic amenities (like private bathrooms) totally sucked. So I began a carefully crafted campaign to tug at the heartstrings of the 'rents. After a week of heart-wrenching letters, I convinced Mom to come and save us.

That's when she told us she and Dad were getting a divorce.

Dad wasn't there at the time. He'd taken the opportunity while we were away at camp to pack up all his things and move to a condo in downtown Chicago, complete with a lake view and a stainless-steel kitchen for his new life with his twenty-five-year-old secretary, Chloe, who turned out to only hold the title of Mrs. Tate for a nanosecond before Dad took up with Carmen. Mom blames Dad's midlife crisis, his BMW convertible, and his new hair-growing Propecia prescription. I blame Dad. He could've at least had the decency to leave us for true love.

After a long plane ride, and then a short one on a small plane with propellers, I find myself at a tiny municipal airport somewhere near the coast of Maine. The last mall I saw was somewhere over Boston. I doubt even Gap.com delivers here. I am so not going to be getting any new clothes for a while. The thought seriously depresses me.

Dad says that if I applied five percent of the time I use to think about clothes and shoes to school, I'd have a 4.0 average. But what fun is a 4.0 if you can't also look hot? Life is about balance.

My current "going to boarding school" ensemble involves: torn jeans, army fatigue cabbie hat, and olive green Juicy Couture tunic tank (bought on eBay on the cheap, but still cost me a month's worth of lunch money and two weekends of babysitting cash). Gold bangles on my wrists and oversize hoop earrings, courtesy of Urban Outfitters.

wuthering high   13

I'm average height, though a bit on the lanky side (lanky = no boobs or hips), and I've got naturally kind of mouse-brown hair, only it's not been that color since I learned how to use Clairol in eighth grade. Current color: dark brunette, like all the blondes-turned-brunette this season (Ashlee Simpson, Mary-Kate Olsen, you get the idea).

The whole wooded area thing is beginning to remind me of camp. Perversely, this gives me hope. I got out of that. I can get out of this.

On the bus to the ferry, I glance around and see some of my classmates. There are boys wearing eyeliner, one guy with bright green hair, and in front of me, a girl who looks like she ought to be starring in the next sequel of *The Ring.* Her hair is hanging in her face in greasy strands. I mean, did she ever hear of a comb? Seriously, gross.

These are my peers. And they are total losers.

Great.

I look away, slipping my hand into my backpack and wrapping my hand around my minican of mace. I've been carrying mace around ever since Tyler tried that stunt in his Toyota. I'm ready if any of these delinquents tries anything.

I put on my headphones to my CD player—another great injustice in my life. All I asked for last Christmas was an iPod Nano. Instead, Mom got me a sweater with stuffed Santa Clauses on it (one that I will not wear in public ever as long as I live), and my dad got me an

Xbox 360. Yes, I know. An Xbox is cool. But I don't play video games. I don't care about blowing up space aliens. All I want is to be able to listen to Death Cab for Cutie without lugging five hundred pounds of CDs around with me everywhere I go.

Besides, Dad wanted the Xbox for himself, but was too embarrassed to admit it to the store clerk, so he had to say it was for me and my sister. But it was Dad who played Halo for four hours on Christmas Day.

Even worse, when I tried to sell the Xbox on eBay, Dad grounded me. Sure, it's a bratty move. But consider this: Dad played the Xbox more than I did. It was clearly a me-to-me gift disguised as a dad-to-daughter gift. I called him on it, and I'm the one who got grounded. How is that fair?

The bus pulls up to a dock by the ocean, and we're directed to board a boat that will take us to Alcatraz Academy. The wind whipping off the Atlantic is strong and cold, and the sign on the ferry says TO SHIPWRECK ISLAND.

Great. The island where I'm going to school is called Shipwreck Island. Why not go ahead and call it Skull Island? Or Dead People Live Here Island? I mean, where am I? A *Scooby-Doo* cartoon?

The brochure in the office where we wait for the ferry says that the island is called Shipwreck Island because of its odd ability to pull in ships during storms, when it was usually hidden by fog. Scores of sailors died when their ships hit the island and sunk. Great. I look at the island in the distance. It's got a bit of fog around it, but I can still tell it's covered in trees. It's not exactly Maui.

The ferry is already full of students who look like the ones on the bus (i.e., delinquents). And they're waiting for us, apparently, before taking off. Once on the boat, it starts off almost immediately, its bell ringing, as kids of all shapes and sizes mingle around the benches. I lean over the rail and look at the black water lapping against the side, and think about jumping. The water looks cold, though. Cold and deep.

Twenty minutes later, we come to rest on the shores of Shipwreck Island with a creak and a lurch. There's no sand on the beach at all—it's entirely rocks. Near us, there's a giant white lighthouse, which is dark. There's only about four feet of rocky beach. After that, it's nothing but thickly wooded trees.

At the dock, there's a shuttle bus waiting for us. It has BARD ACADEMY written on the side. The bald driver—who's wearing a green sun visor, giant amber-shaded aviator sunglasses, and a cigarette in a holder like Cruella De Ville—gruffly grabs my bags and throws them into the storage compartment by the bus door. He's wearing shorts and knee socks. Definitely the weirdest bus driver I've ever seen. On his jumpsuit uniform, his name patch reads "H. S. Thompson."

"You holding?" he asks me in a voice so gruff it sounds as if he's been smoking since he was born, which from the look of him was a long time ago.

"Holding what?" I snap.

He narrows his eyes at me and clenches his teeth around his cigarette holder.

"Never mind," he says. "What are you waiting for? Get in." He mumbles something else under his breath that sounds like "spoiled damn kids. Can't believe I'm stuck here without quaaludes."

Surely, though, I didn't hear him right.

Inside the bus, there are two Goth kids in the back who are smoking clove cigarettes. There's a tough-looking guy who seems ancient—is he like twenty-two?—wearing just a white button-down shirt and plain pants. The shirt has a weird, ruffled collar, like he's just come off the set of *A Christmas Carol,* but everything else about him screams tough guy. In fact, he takes away a lighter from one of the Goth kids. He just takes it straight out of the kid's hand, and starts playing with it himself as if he's never seen a Zippo lighter before. His facial expression says he wouldn't mind lighting the whole bus on fire. He watches me as I get on the bus, but I ignore him. I wonder why I didn't notice him on the ferry.

I take a seat toward the front of the bus, away from the pyromaniac, and mentally, I imagine the first letter I'm going to write my parents.

Dear Mom and Dad:
Thanks for sending me to school with felons and drug dealers. I'm learning all the basic life skills, including setting fire to objects and how to make

deadly weapons out of my hairbrush. I've met my husband-to-be here. He's 28, a pyromaniac, and a convicted felon, but we're in love and we want to get married.

If I play my cards right, my stay at Bard Academy will be no longer than a week.

I glance out the bus window and see the ferry leave. There goes my chance for escape, I think.

Pyro, the guy with the lighter, is staring at me rather intently. Those boots he's got on are weird. Maybe that's the trend among gangbangers this year. Dress like Charles Dickens.

Thompson—the weird driver—slides into his seat, still smoking, and slams the door shut.

"I'd tell you to fasten your seat belts, but there aren't any," he says, grinning mischievously. "So you brats better just hang on to something."

He grounds the gears of the bus and takes off with squealing tires, lurching from side to side, nearly flinging me out of my seat. I watch as he blows right past a STOP sign without even slowing down, and nearly careens into the gates by the port.

Unbelievable. My parents have sent me to Nowhere Island to die. I grab hold of the seat in front of me. The Goth kids blow clove smoke at me and seem unperturbed. Pyro scowls.

This is *so* going in the letter. Thompson has broken at least four rules of the road in the last five minutes, not to mention reckless endangerment of minors. I take a picture of Thompson with my camera phone. He's rummaging around in the glove compartment and not even paying attention to the road. I look at my phone, but his face is all blurred, his features indistinguishable. Odd.

I look at the signal bars on the phone. I get one every now and then, but it doesn't stay long enough for me to make a phone call. I am convinced I'm going to die on this bus.

No one in the bus but me seems at all disturbed by Thompson's driving. I guess they don't have anything to live for.

We drive for what feels like days down a winding, two-lane road. Luckily, we pass no other cars because Thompson is weaving in and out of his lane like my paternal grandma after she's had one too many Amaretto sours. We nearly avoid careening off a cliff when one side of the road crawls up a mountain, giving the guardrail a slight dusting. I'm beginning to feel very car sick. I don't know if it's Thompson's driving or the fact that I'm frantically writing down every new near-death experience in my letter to Mom.

I take a break from writing and watch as tree after tree whizzes by my window. The forest is so thick that it's grown out past the side of the road, over the guardrails, and a few branches are so long that they whip against the windows of the bus.

I don't know where we're going, but I'm pretty sure

it's a filming location for one of the *Friday the 13th* movies. Some crazy people would say that forests and mountains are beautiful, but to me the outdoors are just plain creepy. I see forests and I think of maniacs wielding chainsaws. You never hear of psychotic, crazed killers in movies striking at the mall. No. The freaky killers who turn their victims into wax do it way out in the country somewhere far away from Banana Republic.

After I'm pretty sure that the bus is going to be attacked by ax-wielding psycho killers, we turn off the main street onto a dirt road. You heard me. Dirt road. As in—no pavement. Lovely. My parents are blowing my college tuition on some delinquent academy, and they can't even cough up enough cash for asphalt. I glance at my phone again. Still no reception. Where *are* we? Even at Camp Poison Ivy, I had two bars on my phone.

We're bounced around enough to give us whiplash (and for Pyro to drop his lighted lighter three times), and just when I'm pretty sure I'm going to hurl, we reach the Bard Academy gate—a black metal archway with the Bard Academy logo painted in silver on top. The campus beyond looks like some sort of college brochure. That is, if it was the Crypt Keeper University.

All the buildings are old and Gothic, made of white stone and decorated with gargoyles. God, who designed this place? The Addams Family?

We speed by some groups of students who are wearing the Bard Academy uniform—pleated, navy blue skirts for the girls, navy pants for the boys, both wearing navy blue sweaters with Bard Academy patches on the arm. It's less prep school chic and more military school blech. The pants look like they're made of polyester. I am so not wearing man-made fabrics. Mom, who changes clothes as often as I do, wouldn't approve of artificial fibers, either. There are some things you can sacrifice in the name of personal growth. Breathable fibers isn't one of them.

Thompson comes to a skidding halt in the middle of the neatly kept lawn, two heavy tire marks marring the otherwise pristine commons. The sudden stop sends my backpack skidding forward, and my CD player flies out, along with the battery lid and two Duracells. As Thompson gets up, he steps on the cover, breaking it.

"Hey," I shout at him. "What are you doing!"

"You can't use it here, anyway," he tells me. "Now out with you, you brats."

After I step off the bus, I hear Thompson ask the Goth kids if "they're holding." They hand over a couple of little white pills. Drugs! Our bus driver had been asking if I had any drugs! I don't believe it. Then it dawns on me.

This is awesome.

This is my ticket out of this little horror movie. I am not going to spend even a week here when Dad hears about this. He may not win any Father of the Year awards, but he's got a thing about drugs. In fact, one of his only attempts at parenting involved sitting me down when I was twelve and telling me that alcoholism runs in our family and that I shouldn't try alcohol or drugs because I could get addicted easily.

He told me this as if I didn't notice that Grandma Colleen was always drunk at Christmas, or how she shook before she had her morning cocktail—vodka and orange juice.

I tried to tell Dad he doesn't have to worry about me. I may have tried alcohol, but the key word there is "tried," and given the whole Tyler fiasco, I'm not going back for another round of Everclear anytime soon, thanks. And I'm not going to try any drugs. People on drugs act stupid.

I step off the bus and see what has to be a teacher standing in front of what looks like the campus chapel. He's a burly guy with a white beard wearing what looks like a coach's uniform, complete with cap and whistle. Something about the shape of his head and shoulders reminds me of my dad. I decide instantly that I don't like him. While I watch, he lights up a cigarette, takes a big drag, and then slips his hand into his pocket and takes out a silver flask, which he unscrews and swigs. Wow. Breakfast of Champions, Grandma Colleen style. And he's this school's *coach*? What next? The school nurse is hooked on crystal meth?

He catches me staring at him, and he momentarily lowers his flask. He looks like he recognizes me, but I don't see how that's possible. We've never met.

He stares at me for a beat, taking another drag of his cigarette. He smokes it down to a nub and then drops it underfoot and crushes it.

"Well? What are you waiting for? Inside," he tells me, ushering me toward the church door.

Three

Inside the chapel, it feels colder than outside, which is strange. The walls are covered with stained glass windows, except instead of Christian scenes, they look like scenes from famous books. I recognize the Romeo and Juliet balcony scene, because our school did that play last year. But the others are sort of lost on me. A lot of them have people dying in sword fights. There's serious impaling going on. I'm sure some of the Goth students are in freaky-freak heaven in here.

I'm trying to figure out what religion the chapel is supposed to represent, but as near as I can tell it represents none of them. There aren't any holy symbols, just ones of literature. In fact, above the altar, there's a giant stained glass quill pen picture. Weird. Below the pen, there's a quote from Shakespeare. It says, "I wasted time, and now doth time waste me."

What does that even mean?

I look around at the other students sitting in the pews. They're all in street clothes, and none are in uniforms. There are plenty of Goths and Pyros and Well Girls, but also a surprising number of preps and normal-looking kids. I wonder what they did. Mentally, I try to tick off their offenses. Guy in Red Izod Shirt and Baseball Cap = drug runner because he keeps rubbing his nose and looking around nervously. Thick-necked Jock in Cut-off Tee = date rape. Goth Contingent on the Right = drugs. Christina Aguilera Wannabes with Their Hair Extensions and Too Much Makeup = klepto shoplifters.

I take a seat in a back pew, and Pyro from the bus sits right next to me, completely uninvited. He nods his head in my direction, but says nothing.

I look away from him, a bit unnerved. He has "rebel without a cause" written all over him, despite his weird clothes. Now that I'm closer, I can see that he's definitely older than most of the boys I know. I'm not sure how old, but he seems like he should be in college, not in high school. Look at those sideburns, for heaven's sake. Boys of sixteen don't grow sideburns like that.

Also, now that I'm closer, I notice he's been in a fight. At least, he has a black eye, and a little cut over his eyebrow. Nice. I guess he wanted one last brawl before he was shipped off to reform school.

He's exactly the sort of guy that Dad would freak about—an OMDB Boy. Over My Dead Body Boy.

I'm sure Pyro is only one of *many* Bad Boys in this

boarding school. It would serve Dad right if Pyro and I ended up dating. He's not that bad looking, actually. He's got dark, spiky hair, jet-black eyes, and the beginnings of serious stubble.

The door slams shut then, and beefy guys with Bard Academy T-shirts line the exits. They look like bouncers, or reject college football players, it's hard to say which. Pyro, next to me, gives them all a scowl.

I get the feeling that Pyro likes me for some reason. I try not to judge him on looks alone. When it comes to my peers, I like to think of myself as the secretary general of the United Nations. I don't belong to one group, exactly, but many. At my old school, I had friends in all the cliques—rich kids, smart kids, jock types, geeks— you name it, I know people there. I think it's because I change my look so often. I can go from blonde prep to brunette punk in just about five minutes flat.

I'm not the prettiest girl in my school, or the ugliest, but I do seem to have a sixth sense for trends. You know—what to wear and what not to wear. It's like I can look at a person and make them over—just like Trinny and Susannah—which I did for half the cheerleading squad last year when word got out that I helped Bailey, head cheerleader and prom queen, find the perfect semi-formal dress. It just so happened that we ran into each other in the changing room at Nordstorm. I like to help people, okay? And Bailey, despite her popularity, desperately needed an intervention. I helped her move past sequined mock turtlenecks. Within weeks of the Bailey incident, everybody started asking me for advice. Overnight, I became chief of our campus fashion police.

And it looks like this school is in desperate need of a makeover. I think I am the only person in the room who bothered to accessorize, unless you count tattoos or tongue studs as fashion accessories.

I can feel Pyro's eyes on me. I glance over at him and notice that the cut above his eye is starting to bleed a little bit.

"Are you okay?" I ask him, pointing to my eye and squinting. It looks painful.

He looks surprised that I mentioned it.

He shrugs, but says nothing.

"What did the other guy look like?" I joke, but he doesn't even crack a smile. Tough crowd. "You're sure you're okay? It looks like it hurts. You might need stitches."

"Stitches?" he asks, perplexed, as if he's never heard of them before. Does he have an accent? He sounds like he has an accent. I think it might be English or Scottish. I can't quite tell, but it's definitely Beatles-esque. Cool. I like boys with accents.

"Cathy?" he asks abruptly in his Scottish/English/ Irish brogue.

"Sorry, wrong girl," I say. "My name is Miranda."

He looks a little surprised, like he thinks I might be joking with him.

"Miranda Tate," I say, extending my hand. "And you are?"

He looks at my hand, and then at me. "Heathcliff," he says cautiously, taking my hand. His hand is rough and calloused. Either he's a guitarist, or he's done some hard work on a farm.

"So who's Cathy?"

I watch as a storm cloud moves over his features, then his face settles into a scowl again. He says nothing. I guess it's a sore subject. He doesn't elaborate. Great start I'm off to here at Bard. I try a different tact.

"Where are you from?" I ask him. He glances over at me, scowl still on his face.

"Wuthering Heights," he says.

"Like the book?" I ask him, but he gives me a blank look. He lives in a place called Wuthering Heights and nobody ever told him there's a famous book by the same name?

He falls back into his strong-and-silent routine, so I guess our conversation is over. I look up to the front of the auditorium. On the small stage, a line of what I can only assume are teachers, because they're old and they're dressed badly, files out onto the stage. A tiny but severe-looking woman with jet-black hair parted down the middle and pulled tightly back from her temples steps up to the microphone at the podium, then adjusts it for her height. Some of the kids start snickering.

"I am Headmaster B, and I'd like to welcome you to Bard Academy," she begins in a neatly clipped British accent. Headmaster B? What kind of name is that? Is that because this is our parents' Plan B—to be disciplined by Headmaster B? As I'm thinking this, I notice that she's wearing a broach around her neck on a black ribbon. It's very retro. Like this whole place, actually.

"You suck!" somebody yells.

"Silence!" Headmaster B shouts, and all the doors in the chapel slam shut at once. The lights above our heads flicker.

Wow. That's some party trick. For a full few seconds, no one says a word. Then some students giggle uneasily. Others start booing. The bouncers near the back file down the aisles like storm troopers.

"There will be order," Headmaster B says again. She snaps her fingers and one of the muscle-bound Guardians grabs the nearest kid making noise, wrestles him to the ground, and ties him up like a calf at a rodeo. "Class, it's my pleasure to introduce you to our disciplinary force at Bard Academy, the Guardians."

The muscle-bound guy who has his knee in the back of one rowdy student momentarily straightens and throws up his hand in a kind of salute.

Nice. This boarding school comes with gargoyles *and* prison guards. I can't believe I'm at a school that has its own security force. This is so embarrassing.

I watch as one of the kids in a row near us says "Screw this," and gets up to leave. He's instantly wrestled to the ground, bound, gagged, and put back in his seat. Clearly, he's not the brightest of the bunch.

I make a mental note to put this in my letters home. I think the "Guardians" are clearly violating some Constitutional rights here, like the Constitutional right not to have a 250-pound man put his knee in your back.

"Above me, you will see the motto that we all live by. 'I wasted time, and now doth time waste me.' It's from *Richard II,* and it's a warning to all of us not to waste time. You are here because you wasted your time getting into trouble, but believe me, there will be no wasted time here."

The Guardians hand out packets. I take a stack and pass them on to Heathcliff, who stares at the folder long and hard like he's never seen one before. I wonder if he's high.

Inside the folder, there's a whole book outlining what we can and can't do. Uniforms must be worn at all times beginning "straightaway after orientation." Curfews are enforced daily: 8:00 P.M. for underclassmen, 9:00 P.M. for seniors. All students must sign in at their dorms every day, before their curfew. No going into the woods at night, or ever.

"I would like to draw your attention to page five of *The Student Code of Conduct.* For those of you who are new to Bard Academy, you will find a very important announcement. Every student must earn the right to return home for holidays, such as Thanksgiving and Christmas. You do this by earning good grades and good conduct marks."

What? Hit pause. Rewind. There's a chance I won't be able to go home for Thanksgiving? Or Christmas?

Students across the chapel murmur. I involuntarily

let out a sigh of frustration. One of the Guardians in the aisle gives me a sharp look. Next to me, Heathcliff glares at the Guardian and leans forward a little as if to protect me from the Guardian's gaze. I'm not sure what that's about, but apparently Heathcliff has taken it upon himself to protect me. I guess this is better than killing me.

Headmaster B continues.

"Also on that page, you'll notice that, in the vein of not wasting time, frivolous distractions from your studies are not allowed at Bard Academy. This includes cellphones, pagers, laptops, electronic games."

At this rule, the chapel erupts in protests. Apparently skipping Christmas isn't nearly as bad as going without your PlayStation. The Guardians rough up some of the louder offenders, and then everybody else falls silent. No one wants to become a human pretzel.

"Now," continues Headmaster B, "if boys will file out to the left, and girls to the right, we'll begin the process of checking you in."

As we stand, Heathcliff scowls. He seems reluctant to leave me. For the first time, I notice that he doesn't have any luggage. I've got a rolling suitcase, a backpack, and a Bed-in-a-Bag (Mom's doing). But he has nothing. Just his lighter and the folder they've passed out.

"Um, see you around?" I say to him.

He says nothing, but watches me leave. I can feel his eyes on me the entire way out of the chapel.

Four

"This is totally bogus," complains the girl standing in line in front of me. She's talking in an exaggerated California surfer-girl accent. "I mean, like, oh—my—God, I cannot live without my iPod."

I watch as the guards confiscate mini TVs and DVD players, BlackBerrys, cellphones and Palm Pilots, iPods and Nanos, PSPs, Xboxes, even laptops—basically, anything you can think of that might make life tolerable in the middle of nowhere. Even our hair dryers and curling irons are confiscated, which to me is the worst thing of all. It means that my hair isn't going to be coming out of a ponytail until I leave this place. Not that I have anyone here I want to impress exactly, but it's the principle of the thing.

"Is this school run by the Amish or something?" says someone else behind me. "I am so not giving up my PSP."

I've got a hand-me-down laptop from Dad—it's four

years old and it only does dial-up—but it's a computer anyway, and how else am I supposed to check my e-mail? And I guess I can kiss blogging on MySpace good-bye. My last entry said: "Am off to an island off the coast of Maine. If you don't hear from me in twenty-four hours, call for help." I guess I'll find out how much my MySpace pals really care about me.

The thought of being without e-mail, IM, or MySpace is just too much. Surely there are at least computer rooms here? I mean, it's the new millennium. How are we supposed to do our classwork without computers? Do they expect us to write with quill pens?

I shiver. And what is up with the AC blasting in here? It's freezing. Seriously. It's at least twenty degrees colder in here than it is outside. It's like the dark, Gothic setting just sucks away heat.

I'm getting closer to the end of the line, where Headmaster B is standing. She is watching Guardians search through backpacks and luggage. The bouncers confiscate anything that runs on batteries, as well as "contraband," which includes drugs, CDs, DVDs, games, and magazines.

I inch forward and watch as the surfer girl has her bag searched.

"Do you know who my dad is?" the surfer girl says. "He'll be suing all of you. My psychiatrist says I can't be without my iPod, okay? It's for my mental health."

The Guardians looking through her bags take the iPod anyway.

I slip my mobile flip-phone into the waistband of my jeans and pull my sweater down over it. There's no way I'm going to be without my phone. I don't care what they say about the digital-free zone. There's got to be somewhere on this campus where phones work.

I glance behind me and see a dark-haired girl standing there. She's got long, jet-black hair and a bit of an exotic look about her. Her eyes are nearly black, they're so dark, and she's got smooth, flawless skin. She's also got a sort of thrift-store style that I admire. She's wearing a bunch of clunky necklaces with colored glass beads and black-framed glasses.

"Nice necklace," I say.

"Thanks," she says. She hesitates a minute and then adds, "Hey, if you want to keep that phone, give it to me."

I guess the phone is kind of obviously stuck in my waistband.

"I've got a hiding place," she says, pointing to an interior pocket of her bag. She's got a half-open book in there, except the book has a square cut out of its pages. She already has a few batteries stowed there. I hesitate. Is she going to steal it?

In front of me, a girl is frisked, and a Guardian pulls out an iPod from the back of her jeans. I guess I don't really have a choice here.

I take the phone out of my pocket and put it into her book. She snaps the book shut and then zips up her backpack. I notice she has a lot of books in there. I wonder if they are all hollow.

Before I know it, it's my turn, and the Guardians open my suitcase and rummage through my underwear. Gross.

The Guardians take away my CD player and CDs, which is just as well since the CD player is broken. They look through my coat, and a woman actually frisks me. It's embarrassing. I am so in hate with my parents right now.

While I'm being manhandled, I see the alcoholic coach from outside walk up to Headmaster B. He whispers something in her ear, and then they both look in my direction. I think they're talking about me.

And then, Headmaster B approaches.

"Miranda Tate," she says. It's not a question. "Miranda, Miranda, our innocent young heroine of *The Tempest.*"

This is an odd salutation, but hey, maybe it's what headmasters do. Go around quoting Shakespeare.

"No, I'm Miranda Earnshaw Tate, named after my great aunt on my father's side," I correct.

We read *The Tempest* in English class last year. It's a Shakespeare play where Miranda falls in love with Ferdinand. Guys in my class would make kissy faces to me during all the love scenes. I didn't understand all of the story, but I know Miranda and her father (Prosperous? Prospero? Something like that) were shipwrecked on an enchanted island. Maybe the comparison isn't that far off. I feel more than a little shipwrecked at the moment.

She turns to go, and the guards hand me back my bags and then get started on the one behind me. Headmaster B waves her hand to show that I'm dismissed.

The dark-eyed girl behind me is calm as they look through her bag, not bothering to inspect the books very closely.

Outside the building, the dark-eyed girl speaks.

"Headmaster B seems to be interested in you," she says.

"Is that a good thing?" I ask her.

"Definitely not," the dark-eyed girl says, which makes me laugh. "Here," she says, handing me back my cellphone.

"Wow, thanks." I put the phone in my pocket. "How did you know to do that?"

"This is my second year at Bard," she says, shrugging. "By the way, I'm Hana Mura."

"I'm Miranda," I say.

"Yeah, I heard," she says. I blush a little.

"You're new, right?" she asks me with a cool calmness about the way she's assessing me. I can sense she's normal, unlike the freaks on the bus I rode in with.

"Yeah. Did the 'oh my God, where have my parents sent me' look on my face give me away?"

Hana laughs, and I feel a strange kind of relief. I desperately want her to like me. She's the only normal person I've seen here.

"You're a sophomore, too, right?" she asks.

"How'd you know?"

"The tag on your luggage," she says, pointing to the blue sticker the Guardians put on it. "Come on, I'll show you our dorm."

Hana leads me to Capulet Hall. I learn from Hana that there are two sets of dorms on campus for girls and boys, divided by age. Capulet (freshman/sophomore) and Macbeth (junior/senior) for girls, and Montague (freshman/sophomore) and Macduff (junior/senior) for boys. There are some particularly young-looking girls lingering on the steps of the Capulet dorm, and I wonder what they did to be shipped off to delinquent boarding school. I mean, when I was fourteen I barely got into trouble at all. Not to mention I made it more than halfway through the year after my fifteenth birthday before getting into trouble at all. I'm practically sixteen (March 25—yes, I'm an Aries. Watch out). It dawns on me that there's a chance (albeit remote) that I'll be spending my birthday here. If that happens, I *swear* I will never speak to my parents again.

Like all buildings on campus, Capulet has a pointed roof, and lots of gargoyles.

"Cozy," I say, staring up at the winged monster that's sitting above the door.

"I think it would make a good drinking game," Hana says matter-of-factly. "See a gargoyle, take a drink."

"Around here that's a way to get drunk in a hurry," I say.

"You're down that way," Hana says, pointing down the hall.

"Oh, thanks," I say, as a few white-faced Goths push past us. I feel a stab of disappointment. I'm not sure if I'm ready to wade back into the Sea of Freakdom. I liked the normalness of Hana.

"See you around then," she says, and disappears around the corner.

The door to my room is open. It's got no bathroom, and it's only big enough for two single beds, a single dresser, two tiny closets, and two tiny desks—with lamps.

My roommate has moved in already, and she's decorated her side of the room in what appears to be a uniting theme of . . . Satan.

She's got demonic posters covering every inch of her side of the room, including a black pentacle, a giant picture of the Devil tarot card, and posters of Marilyn Manson. Her shelves are already lined with books about witchcraft, spells, and tarot readings. On her desk sits a life-size skull-shaped candle.

Where did she get this stuff? Pottery Barn: The Hellmouth Collection?

I back out of the room slowly and double-check the number on the outside. Yeah, it's room 216. This is my room, and it's just gotten an Extreme Home Makeover by the Prince of Darkness.

I take a look at the purple-and-pink–polka-dotted comforter under my arm, the Bed-in-a-Bag that Mom bought at Linens-N-Things, and think, I am not in Kansas anymore.

My roommate (whose official name, according to my sign-in sheet, is "Jill Thayer") uncurls herself from the bed. She's got orange-and-black hair, which she's wearing in pigtails, as well as four rings through her eyebrow, one through her nose, and a giant tattoo of a spider on her shoulder. She's wearing enough black eyeliner to graffiti a 7-Eleven.

"Um, hi?" I say, not sure what it is you're supposed to say to a punk-Marilyn Manson-Satan worshiper.

She holds up a notepad. She's written on the page, "I have taken a vow of silence."

She flips the page and it says, "I am protesting my imprisonment against my will here and will not be speaking to you or anyone else."

I nod. Okay. She's a Satan worshiper *and* she is freakin' crazy. On the bright side, she's not going to be making much noise.

She flips the page: "P.S. Don't touch my stuff." I look around at the giant skull candle she's got on her desk, her Satan poster, and the black-and-red quilt on her bed that is covered with pentagrams drawn in permanent marker. Yeah, I think there's absolutely zero chance I'll be touching any of her stuff.

She hands me a printout of her MySpace profile.

NAME: Blade Thayer
TURNONS: Marilyn Manson, throwing
things at little kids, weirdos, writing
poetry, being handcuffed, witchcraft.

TURNOFFS: Liars, fakes, flakes, crazy bitches (that try to mess up your life 'cause they don't have one), people who freakin' stare, and anyone who calls me Jill. The name is BLADE. I had it legally changed.

Before I'm done reading, she snatches it away from me and then goes back to her bed, where she curls up again into the fetal position. There's no reason to ask her why she's here. It's pretty obvious that she wouldn't fit into any normal high school. Can you say Freak with a capital F?

I put my bag on my bed and start unpacking. It's a bit odd with Blade (why not Hatchet or Steak Knife?) curled up in a ball and facing the opposite wall, but after a while, I just decide to ignore her. I open my closet, where I find a row of identical Bard Academy uniforms. I shove them aside to make room for my real clothes. Mom would only let me pack a few outfits, because that's what the Bard Academy guide suggested. I've brought: jeans, my favorite Lucky Brand hooded sweatshirt, a dress (in case of dance/date potential), a couple of baby doll tees, and my favorite flannel Boys Stink PJs. I turn off the light and then turn my attention to the bed. I put sheets on it, and then I take out the framed pictures I brought with me—one of me and Dad, one of me, Mom and Lindsay, and one of my two best friends (Liz and Cass).

Dad's got his sunglasses on and he's smiling because we're on the golf course. That was the summer Dad gave me golf lessons for my birthday. The lessons were a disaster (I threw the golf club farther than I hit the golf ball) but the picture is a good one. It's the only one I have of Dad when he's with me and he's smiling. Every other picture he looks bored, or worse, annoyed.

I get sad when I look at this picture. More than a little sad—like almost choked-up sad, which is ridiculous. I'm not normally sentimental, especially not about Dad, but the picture suddenly makes me feel very alone.

I put it down and pick up the next one to distract me (I am not going to cry over Dad—especially not now). The third picture is me at my fifteenth birthday. Liz (boy-crazy drama queen) and Cass (rock-star-in-training) are making funny faces, because they are total goofballs I've known since I was four. If I'd met them in high school, we wouldn't have been friends because we hang out with different crowds, but somehow we've stayed friends all this time, despite the fact that Cass listens to Audioslave and can slug a beer in one gulp, and Liz's dream is to be this year's homecoming queen (a goal she's attempting to achieve by sleeping with half of the football team). I think I'm her last remaining virginal friend.

My parents think they're bad influences on *me*, but the truth is that I'm a good influence on *them*. I'm the one who talks Cass back from the ledge when she wants to do tequila shots at a keg party, and I'm the one who convinced Liz to try waiting until the third date before offering the blow job. I'm the one who keeps my friends sane. But do I get points for this? No. I get sent off to reform school.

Still, Liz and Cass are loyal and supportive, and I miss them worse than caffeine, which by the way I haven't had since I snuck some of Mom's coffee earlier this morning. When they heard about my Bard Academy exile, Liz and Cass both offered to hide me in their respective attics. I should've taken them up on their offer.

Looking at the framed pictures on my desk makes me suddenly and desperately homesick. My anger at my parents melts away a little bit as I take in my side of the room, which is pretty bleak and has nearly no decorations, since I didn't think to pack any. It's just my polka-dot bedspread, my pictures, my pink towels, and my Paul Frank monkey robe.

I glance over at Blade's side of the room and wonder how I'm going to sleep with a giant poster of the tarot Devil staring at me all night. I look up and see that my closet light is back on. That's weird. I thought I turned it off. I glance over at Blade, who's still lying on her bed. She couldn't have turned it back on. Could she?

I walk back over and flick the light switch off.

There's a knock on my door. I look up and see Hana.

"Hey," she says, her eyes widening as she sees Blade's shrine to all that is evil. "Uh, wow, that's some room."

Blade rolls over and scowls at Hana.

"There's a meeting downstairs," Hana says, looking at me. "Our dorm mother, Ms. W, is calling it and everyone has to go."

Blade scribbles something furiously on her notepad and then shows it to us. It says, "Down with the fascists!" and is underlined three times, and then she goes back to her bed where she lies down, facing the wall.

"Ms. W?" I say. "What's up with the names at this school? No one has a full name—everybody goes by an initial?"

"I heard it was for the teachers' safety, so that students can't find them in the summer and beat them up."

"You're serious?" I ask her, wondering, again, where on earth my parents have sent me. Rikers for juveniles?

"It's the rumor," she says. "So? You coming?"

I look at Blade. "Definitely," I say.

"What's with her?" Hana asks me when we're out the door.

"That's Jill Thayer, but she's legally changed her name to 'Blade.' She's taken a vow of silence. Her hobbies include selling her soul to Satan, piercing her nose, and being freakin' weird."

"You should totally call her Swiss Army," Hana says, which makes me laugh.

Five

Our dorm mother, Ms. W, calls to order our meeting in the dorm den, a smallish library with couches, chairs, and a giant fireplace. Even though a fire is roaring, the room still feels cold—like every room at Bard. A group of preppy-looking girls wearing nothing but Juicy Couture from head to toe have all the best and most comfortable seats staked out. A few other freaky Goth types occupy the remaining seats. It's standing room only, as Hana and I take up positions near the door.

Ms. W claps her hands. "Let's get settled, everyone," she says in a clipped British accent. I wonder just how many teachers here are British. "I really hate the goons—I mean, Guardians—but I will call them if I must."

Ms. W seems like the sort of teacher who could be okay. The sort who understands there's more to life than school. She's got her hair cut short in a bob and is wearing a dress with a dropped waist. She's got an unfortunate nose, but then, you have to give her points for not dressing like everybody else.

"As you probably know by now, our dorms are a little . . . odd," Ms. W says. "They take some getting used to. I think they're cold and creepy, but that's just me."

Given that my roommate could be a spawn of Satan, I agree with this assessment.

I raise my hand. "When do I get my hair dryer back?"

"Sorry, Ms. Tate," says Ms. W, shaking her head. "Not until you leave. You'll have to learn how to survive without it."

Great.

"This is just as well," Ms. W says. "You girls need to start working on your inner selves, and worry less about your outer selves."

I'm not so sure about that. I glance down at Ms. W's sleeve and notice that it seems to be wet. That's a little strange. Did she spill something on her dress? Maybe she ought to worry a little bit more about her outer self.

"At ten P.M., you'll hear the Bard tower clock toll ten times, and this is your signal to turn off the lights in your room. Anyone caught with lights on after ten will be subject to detention or other punishment. These aren't my rules, people. The headmaster—you met her—she's the one with the Napoleon complex . . ."

A few people giggle at this. It's true, she is *very* short but very stern.

". . . well, you think she'll punish you if you step out of line, but I'll get even worse. So we're all stuck here, in the same predicament. Let's make the best of it, shall we?"

Ms. W sees me staring at her sleeve. She glances down, notices the wet spot, and deftly hides her hand behind her back. Odd.

"So I'm sure you all have memorized the rules and regulations by now," she continues. "Normally, dinner is served at six, but tonight dinner will be late—in about an hour."

"What happens if we don't make curfew?" someone shouts.

"I have to turn you in to the Guardians, and they are very grumpy at night," she says. "There typically is dish duty or toilet cleaning involved. Trust me, girls, you don't want to have to do this."

There are groans in the room.

"And everybody here should really be kissing up to me," she continues, "because I'm the person who says if you go home for Thanksgiving or not. Now, I'm from England and we don't celebrate Thanksgiving. That is just for you Yanks. But, I'll take cash donations, or just worship. I don't mind worship. By the way, each of you will be meeting with me once a week to talk about how things are going. And just to talk about things in general."

There are groans around the room. Apparently, the idea of counseling doesn't appeal to this group.

"One last thing—your first few nights at Bard are going to be difficult ones. If you have something you want to talk to me about—and believe me, I'm sure you will—let me know. I don't sleep very much, so just knock on my door if you need to. It's the one right by the front door, so don't think about trying to run off. I hear everything," she says.

There are a few sighs and grunts to this.

"All right, girls," Ms. W says. "You're dismissed."

The other girls start to file out, including Hana. I feel a sudden urge to try to reason with Ms. W, so I linger behind. I don't belong here. I mean, I *really* don't belong here.

"Ms. W," I say, reaching out to touch her sleeve, but when I do, I feel that it is, indeed, wet. Not just damp, but soaking. I'm surprised it's not dripping. It's like before-the-spin-cycle wet.

Ms. W whips her sleeve from my hand.

"Can I help you, Ms. Tate?" she asks. "Here to ask me more about blow-dryers? Or do you have a more substantive question?"

"There's been some mistake. I mean, I really don't think this is where my parents intended to send me. I don't belong here. This is all some big, *big* mistake."

Ms. W looks a bit sad. "Trust me when I tell you that I've been here a lot longer than you, and want to leave a lot more."

This might be sarcasm, but she sounds like she's a

prisoner, too. But isn't she an adult? Can't she leave anytime she wants to?

"But, Ms. W., I mean it, I really, *really* don't belong here."

She puts her hand on my shoulder and gives me a little pat. Her hand is so cold, I can feel the chill through my shirt. "I'm sorry, Miranda. There's not much I can do."

"But . . ."

"It's out of my hands," Ms. W says, shrugging, as she walks out of the den. I look down and notice that she's left a trail of wet footprints. They follow her out the room and down the hall.

I glance at the window outside. There's no rain. Not even a cloud in the sky. And I look around the floor for a puddle, or something that might account for the water, but everything except her footprints is dry.

Odd.

Back in my room, Blade lights some incense that smells a lot like goat, and then begins some kind of silent dance in the middle of our room.

"Um, do you have to do that?" I ask her when her flying elbow nearly hits me in the face.

She furiously scribbles "Sacred Wiccan Protection Vampire Ritual" on her notepad and shows it to me, and then points to the wall. In one of the spaces not covered by a picture of Satan or his minions, there is a certificate that reads, "Wiccan Witch, Certified 2003 by Wicca Women's Association—Cleveland."

"Vampires? What do you mean?"

She picks up an old copy of *Dracula* from her desk and hands it to me.

"I know what a vampire is," I say, pushing the book aside. "But why are you protecting us from them?"

She scribbles on her notepad, "Saw one," as if this is a regular occurrence for Blade. You know, some people go bird watching. Blade prefers vampire watching. Now I know she's insane.

She tries to hand me a string of garlic to wear around my neck, but I decline. I don't really want to smell like a lasagna, thanks.

Blade shrugs and then leaves the room, wearing her own garlic lei.

I decide I've had enough.

I undo the latch at the window and find it swings inward. I look out and see I'm on the third floor, but there's a ledge, and even better, a drainpipe. Just like the one at home I used (once!) to sneak out of my room.

Could it be this easy? Could my ticket to freedom be right in front of me? I glance back over my shoulder and decide I'm not going to wait for Blade to come back. I grab my backpack and put my foot on the ledge. I come face-to-face with a gargoyle and nearly lose it. Jesus. Why does this place have to be so freakin' creepy? God! I put my hand on its head and haul myself out the window.

I climb halfway down and then jump the rest of the way. I land on the ground hard, but manage not to hurt anything. It's not that much different than sneaking out of my room at home. Not that I've done that more than once or, okay, maybe twice. And I swear it's all Cass's fault (I guess in some ways she *is* the Bad Influence Friend—she always knows of the kegger party, and always wants me to come).

I march off in the direction of the woods. Can you really blame me? The bus driver nearly killed me, there are brain-dead Guardians beating the hell out of anybody who breathes, the students are insane (see Blade and Heathcliff), and I am being forced to live without a hair dryer. I don't know what other signs you need. I've seen Lifetime Original Movies (or as Cass calls them, Knifetime Original Movies, because of how often a deranged, knife-wielding stalker pops up in one of them). I'm not going to wait around to be a Knifetime victim.

There don't seem to be any teachers or other adults about as I make my way down by the buildings and toward the dirt road that the bus took to get here. I'm not an outdoors girl, so I think it's best if I stick with roads. Just as I'm almost to the Bard Academy gate, I see two Guardians walking by. Quickly, I duck into the forest. The sky above me is a dark shade of magenta. It's starting to get dark. I wonder how often that ferry comes. Hopefully, often.

I try to remember what they told us about surviving in the woods at night at camp. I didn't pay attention. I never imagined I'd actually have use for camping survival types. Who knew?

I start heading in the direction where I think the

road is. I walk for what seems like forever. I'm getting a blister on my right toe and I'm now ankle-deep in what has to be poison ivy. Mosquitoes buzz in my ear and nip at my arms. I've smashed two already and missed a half dozen more. Bugs of some kind are nipping at my ankles. Knowing my luck today, they're probably ticks. I'll not only be lost in the woods forever, but I'll also contract Lyme disease.

I try imagining the speech I'm going to give my parents when I call them whenever I finally get someplace where my mobile phone works. Mom will have to listen about the "no hair dryer" rule and polyester uniforms. Then she'll have to take me back. Sure, she wants to punish me, but even she can't want me to be without my hair dryer. Good grooming is a basic civil right.

I run into yet another spiderweb and I do that really embarrassing Spiderweb Dance. Liz says that when people run into a spiderweb they always do the same thing—flail their arms and do a little boogie dance, which makes everyone, no matter how cool they are, look ridiculous. I think about Liz talking about the Spiderweb Dance and have to smile. I miss her. I miss Cass, too. I can't believe I didn't take them up on their offer to stow me away in their attics.

While I'm struggling with the spiderweb, I nearly run smack into another tree branch. The forest is getting thicker. And it's definitely getting darker. I should've been to the road by now. I don't remember it being this far.

Something rather large rumbles around in the bushes a few yards away.

If that's a chipmunk, it's a really big freaking chipmunk.

I start thinking again about the *Friday the 13th* movies. I never should've watched them when they came on cable. Now look at me. I'm worried about a psycho killer in the woods on some island off the coast of Maine.

Another mosquito bites my arm. I smack it, and think I shouldn't be worried about Jason. I should be worried about contracting malaria.

I see lights up ahead. The road—finally. Jeez. It's taken me long enough.

I check my mobile phone: still no bars, but the phone says I've been walking for an hour.

I push the last branch away from the lights and find myself staring, not at the road, but at the white stone buildings of Bard Academy. In fact, it's the exact place I stepped into the woods.

This is impossible.

I look around. How did this happen? I could've sworn I wasn't moving in a circle. I'm an outdoors virgin, but still, I've got a better sense of direction than this. I never get lost in the mall, ever. Could the woods be so different?

And even if I did get lost, how did I come back at the *exact spot* where I left? I mean, that's just not possible that I did a U-turn somewhere out there. But here I am, right back in the Goth Village, right in front of the lion statues standing guard outside the library.

The campus is eerily quiet. And I notice that even though we're on an island, I don't hear the sound of the ocean. Everything is quiet, except, in the distance, a wolf howls.

This isn't normal.

Just *where* am I?

Six

When I get back to the dorm, I find it completely empty.

What the . . . ?

The halls and every room is empty. Completely deserted. What happened? Where is everybody? I wander into the dorm den, where I find Ms. W sitting by the fire and reading a book.

The wet spot on her sleeve is gone, but there seems to be one near the hem of her dress. Odd.

She closes her book and looks at me.

"Got escape out of your system, I hope," she says, in clipped English.

I flinch. "How did you—?"

"I have my ways," she says. "Not including the mud that you have all over your jeans."

I look down at them and can feel my face go red. I guess I have to work on being more stealth.

"I'm sorry, I am, it's just that . . ."

"The woods are dangerous, you know," she tells me as I watch a single drop of water fall from the hem of her dress and land on the carpet. Is it water or sweat? "You could've died of hypothermia, or worse."

I don't think I want to know what "worse" is.

"And even if you made it out of the woods, where are you going to go? We're on an island, Miranda," she says. "The ferry only comes twice a day."

She has a point.

I realize that she at least cares about my welfare. It's more than I can say about my dad.

"I'm sorry," I say, and mean it.

"I could turn you in, but I'm not going to. This is your one free pass, you understand me?" I nod. She looks at her watch. "Now you're late for dinner. Change into your uniform and head to the cafeteria before all the food is gone."

"I am not going out in public like this," I say to my reflection in the mirror after I've changed.

I look down at myself and all I can see is old-school Britney Spears. I've got on a white starched shirt, which makes my already nonexistent boobs even more nonexistent, along with a navy blue skinny tie with the Bard Academy seal on it, and a short, pleated Bard Academy skirt. To complete the ensemble: white knee-high socks. All I need are pigtails and some dance moves and I am the pre–Federline Britney. If anyone I knew ever saw me in this, I'd literally die of embarrassment. I have a fashion reputation to protect. I should be singing "Oops, I Did It Again."

I am already thinking about ways I can try to make it cooler. Maybe if I shredded the hem, or the tie? Anything would be an improvement. I put on my navy blue cap (the one Lindsay calls my Fidel Castro hat, because it's square and has a short brim) and some bangles and dangle earrings, which is the best I can do on short notice.

The dining room is dark and depressing. The lights above are dimly lit chandeliers, with flickering bulbs that give off about as much light as candles. The electricity in the dining hall and about everywhere else seems patchy at best. The lights keep flickering.

The walls are all dark-paneled wood and the room is filled with long, wooden tables paired with benches that are bolted to the floor. No plastic chairs here. I wonder if this is to prevent students from throwing them. I head to the line, where I am the next-to-last person to get my tray and get my food.

Calling the meal they serve us "dinner" is being generous. Even calling it "food" would be something of a stretch. On the bright side, I'm pretty sure I'll be able to drop fifteen pounds without even trying.

The meal, if you want to call it that, consists of a big white roll (um, carb-heavy, no thanks), some mystery meat swimming in some unidentifiable gravy, and green beans so soggy they disintegrate on the fork.

I'm not sure what's scarier. The woods, my polyester uniform, or this food.

Have these people ever heard of Cheetos? Cap'n Crunch? Something edible? I take my tray to the end of the line and then look for a place to sit.

Amazingly, everyone seems to be sitting in groups of friends already. It's not even the first day of classes and already there are cliques. Where did they come from? Was there a meeting I missed? There are literally no singles sitting at any table. Everyone is at least paired up with someone else, and here I am, alone in a sea of unfamiliar faces. I literally see *no one* I recognize. Not even Blade. I feel my heart sink.

I wait a beat or two, counting down the seconds as I stand with my tray, glancing around the cafeteria. I realize that I'm quickly slipping from the "casually looking for friends" zone into the "this girl has no friends and doesn't know where to sit" zone. I glance up and see a guy with a pink Mohawk, who nods at me. Does he want me to sit with him?

Oh God. Am I reduced to sitting with Pink Mohawk Guy? Seriously? Is this my life now?

And then, a punkish girl with green hair steps out of line behind me and heads to the Pink Mohawk Guy. He wasn't nodding at me, he was nodding at Green Spiky Hair Girl. Great. Not even the Pink Mohawk Guy wants me to sit with him. I don't think I can sink lower.

Get a grip, I tell myself. It's not that bad to sit by yourself, is it? Besides, is it so bad to be a social pariah at Bard? I mean, what does it say about you if you're popular at a school of delinquents? Yeah, thought so. This rationale makes me feel instantly better. I'm not a social pariah; if anything, being an outcast here makes me normal.

Then I see someone I recognize. It's Hana. And she's sitting with a boy. Oh, thank God! I'm saved. I catch her eye and she gives me a smile. I'm in.

"Hey, mind if I sit with you guys?" I ask, approaching them.

"Sure, have a seat," Hana says, nodding to the seat in front of her.

"Thanks," I say. "You saved me."

"You owe me one," Hana says, but she smiles at me. "Miranda, meet Samir. Samir, Miranda."

Samir is slim with an olive complexion and jet-black hair that's a bit unkempt. He seems not to care that his shirt is half tucked-in and half tucked-out of his pants. He looks like he just rolled out of bed.

"Will you marry me?" he asks me.

"Uh . . ." I glance at Hana.

"He asks every girl he meets," Hana explains. "Don't worry about it."

"I'm what you call desperate," Samir says.

"His parents want to arrange his marriage for him," Hana says. "They sent him here because he refuses to get married to the girl of their choice when he turns nineteen."

"That's a little young to get married, isn't it?"

"My parents grew up in India in a very traditional family. They have a different way of thinking about things," Samir says. "So why are you here? Did your parents send you away for telling them you won't have an arranged marriage, too?"

"No, but they could have. My parents are dorks," I say.

"And?"

"And what?"

"What did you do?"

"Samir! Stop being so nosy. Miranda, you don't have to answer that if you don't want to."

"She's right, you know," Samir says. "We can just look it up in your file when you aren't around."

"Ignore him, seriously," Hana says.

"So? Come on. Can't be that bad. You look too goody-goody for it to be that bad. Wait, let me guess. Eating disorder?"

"Just what are you trying to say?"

"Shoplifting. Must be."

"Not even close."

Hana and Samir stare at me. I sigh. I've never been good at doing the whole mysterious thing. "Fine. I wrecked my dad's car. Maxed-out my stepmom's credit card."

"Sweet, right here," Samir says, putting up his hand for a high five. Despite myself, I smile and slap his palm. Samir has a kind of contagious energy. He makes everything seem like a game. "That's almost as good as

Hana's story. She wrecked her mother's car, too. But you know all about Asian drivers."

"First off, I'm only half-Japanese," Hana says, flinging her soggy roll at him. "And second, by that logic, you should be driving a cab."

"Maybe I will," Samir says.

"And anyway, I didn't wreck her car. My boyfriend did."

"You mean your *felon* boyfriend did."

"He wasn't a felon when I was dating him. That was after," Hana clarifies.

I try cutting the mystery meat, but I'm not getting anywhere with this plastic fork. I'd be better off using chopsticks.

"What's with the plastic utensils?" I ask, holding up a fork.

"Someone got stabbed last year," Samir says, unperturbed.

"Stabbed? Seriously?"

"It wasn't very deep," Hana says. "Some guy went ballistic on his roommate. Stabbed him in the arm with his fork. He tried to stab Ms. W, too, but missed."

"He didn't miss," Samir says. "He hit Ms. W right in the forearm, but she didn't bleed. Everybody knows that story. She's an alien. Everybody knows it."

"That is totally just a campus legend," Hana says.

"Campus legend?"

"Bard's version of urban legends," Samir says. "Like the faculty don't eat or sleep."

"Or like the one about the UFO that crashed in the

forest that keeps giving out that weird magnetic pulse, which makes people walk in circles out there."

"That's funny you should say that, because I went into the woods, and . . ."

Both Samir and Hana drop their forks and their mouths hang open.

"You went into the woods!" they both cry at once in raised voices. A couple of other people look at us, and two Guardians standing by the mashed potatoes line glare in our direction.

Hana lowers her voice. "Baring the fact that if you were caught," Hana says, looking from one direction to the other to make sure she's not overheard, "you'd get grounded here for Thanksgiving *and* Christmas, not to mention dish duty for the semester, there's the problem of . . ."

"Bears," Samir says.

"And . . ." Hana starts.

"And wolves, don't forget the wolves," Samir adds.

"And . . ."

"And the ghost of Kate Shaw."

"Would you let me finish my story?" Hana shouts.

"Who's Kate Shaw?"

"The best campus legend," Samir asks.

"I'm telling the story," Hana says, giving him a stern look. "Kate Shaw," she continues, "was a sophomore who came to Bard several years ago. Just like you, Kate Shaw tried to escape. They sent out a search party the next morning looking for her . . ."

"You're not telling it right," Samir says. "You left out the part about her backpack."

"If you'd *let* me finish, I was getting to that part." Hana glares at Samir, who just shrugs. "So she took her backpack, right? They searched for her for five days. And on the fifth day, they found her backpack in the woods by a stream. And it was covered in blood."

"You are *so* telling this wrong," Samir says. Hana ignores him.

"And it was empty, except for one book and a note. The note was covered in blood, and it said, 'Beware the Third Bell.'"

"She was telling people not to be tardy?" I ask.

Samir laughs. "Hana, you're forgetting that they also found her Bard jacket and it was—"

"Wait, let me guess. Covered in blood?" I'm not scared at this point. Just amused.

"And sometimes, late at night," Hana says, continuing even though I'm clearly not scared, "people have seen her ghost wandering the woods and asking people if they've seen her backpack."

"It's much scarier when I tell it," Samir tells me.

"It would've been fine if you hadn't interrupted," Hana says.

The lights above our heads flicker.

"What's with the lights?" I ask them.

They shrug. "The island is powered by a generator," Samir says. "But it's not exactly like being plugged into General Electric."

"Okay, so now back to noncampus legends and real-campus people," I say. "Who are those people?" I nod my head toward a table two over from us. It's filled with Goth types, complete with black lipstick and spiky black hair. "What's their story?"

"Those are the E/rave kids. They're always connected, even in here, with drugs."

"And them?" I ask, pointing to what looks like the jock table.

"Impulse-control problems. Those guys steal everything that isn't nailed down," Hana says.

"And nearly all of them have probably hit one of their parents," Samir says.

"What about them?" I ask, looking over at what must be the geek table, where Well Girl from the bus is sitting.

"The freaks? They're the harmless ones. They aren't trying to be social outcasts, they're just that way naturally. They look all weird, but they don't really want to harm anybody but themselves. There are a lot of cutters over there."

"Gross," I say, wrinkling my nose.

"Yeah, it's pretty much the rainbow of problems here. Do their parents send them to therapists? No, they send them to a prison school, hoping it'll all work out. Does that make sense to you?" Samir points his fork at me for emphasis. "But, like Headmaster B says, we're all here because we have self-esteem issues."

"Ugh," Hana says, rolling her eyes. "Everything here is about self-esteem."

"But what about them? They look normal," I say, nodding toward a table full of people wearing Izod shirts.

"Oh no, they're the *worst*," Hana says. "They're the rich kids. They tend to fall into the "Daddy got my drug/date rape charges dismissed because he knows the DA" category. They're the worst criminals here by far. The ring leader is sitting in the middle with the ponytail. That's Parker Rodham, a junior. She poisoned her own mother with rat poison, or so the rumor goes."

"The mother lived, but she lost a kidney," Samir says.

"Seriously?"

"That's the rumor," Hana says. "Also, all of Parker's boyfriends keep dropping off the face of the earth. We think she kills them."

"Speaking of, looks like Parker found a replacement boyfriend in record time," Samir says, as a blond boy who looks like he ought to be on the cover of a J. Crew catalog takes a seat next to Parker.

With a jolt, I realize I know him.

Ryan Kent, former star of the varsity basketball team at my old school. He was one year ahead of me. He was a sophomore at my school last year, until he had that car accident. His girlfriend was killed and he dropped out of school. Rumor had it he finished up his sophomore year at some private school in the Northeast. Looks like that school is Bard Academy.

I did not just get so lucky. This changes everything. I'm going to have to rethink my guyatus.

"Ryan Kent," I exclaim, without meaning to. Both Samir and Hana look at me.

"You know him?" she says.

"Uh-huh," I mutter, unable to stop staring. Even in his Bard uniform, you can just make out the outline of his state-championship triceps. It's not possible for him to be more gorgeous. And if that's not enough, he's also an honors student. Brains and brawn. Things are definitely looking up. This is the first good news I've gotten since landing at Bard.

"Parker always does snatch up the best-looking boys," Hana says, just as Parker leans in and whispers something into Ryan's ear.

Okay, maybe I spoke too soon about things looking up.

"They can't be dating," I say, as my eyes slide back to Ryan and Parker.

"Why not?"

"I don't know," I say, watching Parker rub Ryan's arm possessively. "They just can't be."

Seven

After dinner, I find Blade asleep in our dorm room. She's found my stash of pretzels from the plane in my backpack and chowed down on them because there are empty wrappers on my bed. Nice. She's laid out on her back and snoring. Apparently, stealing my stuff has really worn her out. I take the wrappers from my bed and toss them onto her chest. One of them flitters near her face. She swats at it, then rolls over and starts snoring soundly again.

I slip into my pajamas and crawl into bed, too. I stare at my photos for a while. I keep looking at Dad's picture, although I don't know why. It's like I'm trying to figure him out. What about *this* day made him smile, when he never smiles any other time? I wonder how he found out about this place? Maybe it was one of his annoying golf buddies, like Mr. Lorgan who stares at my butt when he thinks I don't see. Perv.

The bell outside starts tolling, signaling lights out.

It's then that I notice that my closet light is on again. I slip out of bed, and turn it off, then climb back into bed and switch off my desk lamp. The room feels suddenly colder than it did before, now that it's nearly completely dark. I pull the covers high up to my chin and stare at the ceiling. I'm acutely aware of the weird sounds in my room. There's the snoring from Blade, a kind of wheezing whine, and the eerie creaks and groans of the floorboards above my head. It sounds like someone is walking above me, but they shouldn't be, since we're all supposed to be in bed.

The furthest thing from my mind is sleep. The wind howls against my window and every so often a tree branch outside hits it just right so that I think someone is out there tapping on it. I've never felt so out of place and alone before. I would probably have better luck sleeping in a deserted and haunted mineshaft or maybe a cursed Indian burial ground. Not that I'm the sort of person who believes in ghosts, but it's hard not to think something is weird about this place. If there is such a thing as spirits, this is the place they'd be.

I have got to find a way out of here.

But even if I did manage to escape, where would I go? My parents think I'm a delinquent. Especially Dad. God, he's so clueless. If he spent five minutes with me he might actually *know* something about me. If you quizzed him on my friends' names, I bet he couldn't come up with a single one.

When he and Mom were still married, at least Mom

would tell him things about me, so he'd know some-thing. I miss those days, I guess, even though it wasn't all a big Disney movie or anything. They fought all the time, and usually Dad traveled a lot for work and wasn't around much, but at least back then Mom wasn't obsessed with her wrinkles and Dad wasn't completely preoccupied with golf. And every so often, I felt like we were a family. Now I just feel like I'm in the middle of a battlefield all the time. And just when I thought things couldn't get worse, they send me away, a hundred miles away from my friends and everything I loved about my life. It's like Dad wasn't just content with ruining our family. He had to ruin my whole life, too.

I'm starting to feel pretty sorry for myself, which is what usually happens when I think about Mom and Dad splitting up. I don't know why, because, I mean, people's parents get divorced all the time. It's more the rule than the exception, isn't it?

I feel a lump in my throat and I suddenly feel like I might cry.

Before I can, my closet light flicks on. I start, sitting up in bed. The light from inside the closet outlines the door, sending slashes of light across my bedspread.

What the . . . ?

My heartbeat kicks up a few notches. It's been a long while since I thought there might be monsters hiding in my closet, but I've never seen a light just come on by itself before. I'm temporarily paralyzed. Do

I get up and investigate? I'm not exactly all that thrilled about investigating an odd light coming from the closet. I'm no horror movie virgin. I know what happens to the curious. It starts out as a weird closet light coming on and ends up with me being hacked to pieces.

Cue tense horror music.

Then I remember that we're not allowed to have any lights on after lights out. If somebody sees that closet light, it'll mean detention, or worse.

Reluctantly, I throw the covers off and try to pretend like I am not freaked, when really I am. A little. Okay, more than a little. Even though I know it's probably just a bad lightbulb, right? Or a faulty electrical switch. This place is ancient, so I bet the wiring isn't too new. It is *not* a ghost. Or a serial killer. Or Jason. Or . . . man, I need to stop trying to think of scary things.

I get to the closet, and just when I'm about to open the door so I can turn off the light, something cold touches my shoulder.

"Aaaaaaaaaah," I cry, jumping, I swear, six feet straight up in the air. If this were a scene in a movie, it would be the exact moment you spilled your popcorn all over your knees.

"Ms. Tate," comes the stern voice of Ms. W behind me. She's the one responsible for taking twenty years off my life. "I thought I warned you about lights out."

"But it's not my fault. I was trying to turn it off," I say.

Ms. W steps in between me and the closet, reaching an arm into the closet and turning the light off.

"Time for bed," she says.

I climb back into bed, feeling like a moron. I was scared of a light and Ms. W. I have got to get a grip.

Before I know it, I'm crying. I'm like Mom crying at commercials. What's wrong with me? I shut my eyes, trying to hold back my tears, but they leak out anyway, pooling on my pillow.

Eight

That night I dream there's a huge thunderstorm, so loud it rattles the windows of our tiny dorm room. In the dream, I'm standing at the window, watching the lightning. As I'm watching the raindrops splatter and flatten against the windowpane, something big and shadowy moves outside. Before I know it, the shadow comes toward me, through the window, and glass is flying everywhere. It's a giant tree branch, whipped up by the wind. I wrap my hands around the branch and push it out again, but as I do so, I realize the branch has turned into human hands and they're clutching my wrists. They belong to a girl floating outside the window. She's pale and creepy and her mouth is moving, and she's asking to be let in. And she looks a lot like . . . me.

I sit up in bed, my heart racing and cold sweat trickling down my back. The first thing I see is Blade's poster of Satan and I almost scream. But then I remember where I am. Hell on Earth—Bard Academy. The grayish light of dawn seeps in through the window and I don't know what time it is, but it's definitely early.

It takes me a moment to shake off the scary vibe from the nightmare. I rub my face and try to shake off the fright, even though the backs of my legs tingle with pins and needles and my whole body feels wired with adrenaline.

It's freezing in our room and there's also a strong draft. I look up and see that it's because our window is broken.

Just like in my dream.

There are shards on the floor and the windowpane is cracked and hanging from the window frame in jagged pieces.

That is some coincidence.

Suddenly, I don't want to get out of bed. I have the irrational fear that if I do, I'll see the ghost floating outside, her arms extended, drifting into the room.

The next thing I hear is the sound of a bugle, making me start.

It plays that military thing, you know what I'm talking about, the only piece of music ever written for a bugle. This must mean it's time to get up. Not that I could go back to sleep anyway.

Okay, I tell myself. It's just a broken window. There was probably a storm and a tree branch broke it, which is why I *dreamt* it was broken in the first place. That's it. I get up and start picking up shards when I look up and see that my closet light is on.

Again.

I feel a little chill, but then I talk myself out of being scared. The window and the closet—I bet it's all some prank. That explanation seems so rational that I immediately feel better.

I throw the glass shards into the trash and stalk over to the closet and open it. There's nothing inside but my own clothes. I snap off the light again, but this time I notice a carving in the closet floor. I kneel down to take a closer look. It says:

K.S. WAS HERE. 10/31/90.

Wow. 1990. That's old. That's the year I was born.

When I run my hand over the carving, the floorboard seems uneven and even a little unstable, like it might be loose. Without too much effort, I find the seam of the wood and pry the board up. Underneath it, there's a hidden space, and in it there's contraband, 1990 style. The first thing I pull out is a cassette tape player. Talk about old! Cassette tapes! You have to be kidding me. Next, I pull out some long-dead batteries, an ancient Snickers bar, and the ripped-out page from a book.

It's from *Wuthering Heights,* page 139, to be exact. Weird.

There's something else in the hidden space, too. A card—a library borrowing card for the Bard Academy Library.

And it belongs to:

Kate Shaw.

Okay, I had to imagine that I saw that name. It couldn't

be *the* Kate Shaw, a.k.a. Missing Girl, the covered-in-blood campus legend. I look down at the card again. Nope, that's her name. I turn the card over and I see she's also signed it in scrawly, curlicue writing, with a heart for the "a" in Shaw. Kate Shaw.

I get goose bumps on my arms.

"What's that?" Blade, my roommate, asks me, sitting up in bed and rubbing her head and yawning. Apparently, she's abandoned her vow of silence.

I stuff the page and the library card in my backpack. I don't feel like telling my occult-happy roommate that we might be living in the dorm room where the campus' most famous ghost used to live.

"Nothing," I lie. "Just a Bard brochure."

"Hey," Blade says, seeing the broken window for the first time. "Why did you break the window?"

Blade sounds legitimately surprised. I don't think she's that good an actor. I guess she didn't do it, either.

"I didn't," I say, hastily throwing on my Bard uniform. "But . . ."

I'm out the door before I can hear the rest of the sentence. I don't bother with makeup or even with combing my hair. I need to find Hana and Samir.

"The Kate Shaw? She was a real person? I thought it was just a story," Hana tells me when I show her the library card.

"I knew she was real," Samir says. "I knew it. I told you that a friend of my cousin's girlfriend's brother knew her." Samir pauses, then says, "I bet your room is haunted. That's why the closet light came on. Wow, this is *so* cool. We should have a séance in the room. I could invite all the hot freshmen. You know, because girls put out if they're scared."

"You are disgusting," Hana says, wrinkling her nose. "You are a perv. A total mlut, you know that: a man slut."

"You mean, he would be if anyone would have him," I tease.

"Okay, that is not fair," Samir says. "Not fair at all. I'm just a man. We have needs."

"Ignore him," Hana says as she takes the library card from my hands and inspects it. "Wow. I guess she did exist, but it doesn't prove that she disappeared."

"We could find out," Samir says. "By looking her up in the archives at the library."

Nine

The library is what I would imagine the Library of Congress might look like if I'd ever seen it. Aside from two giant lion statues standing guard outside the biggest building on campus next to the chapel, the library has stone pillars outside it and a huge, tiled lobby guarded by a large, round circulation desk. The bookshelves line the building from floor to ceiling, which has to be at least twenty-five-feet high. Long, rolling ladders are at every shelf and the shelves are so crammed with books that high stacks of them are leaning against nearly every shelf, continuing on for as far as I can see. For some reason, the library seems even bigger on the inside than it looks like it should be from the outside. There's something about the immenseness of it that makes you feel small. I get the feeling that if you scream at one end, no one could hear you at the other.

Now, however, the library isn't quiet. It's full of

dozens of students waiting in lines near the front desk, trying to pick up their class schedules.

"You can't get breakfast until you get your schedule," Hana tells me, explaining the lines.

I think about the awful dinner from the night before.

"If you don't get your schedule, does that mean you don't have to eat breakfast?" I ask, ever hopeful.

"Sorry," Samir says. "I already tried that. They make you eat it, anyway."

"Crap," Hana exclaims suddenly. "We can't get up to see the old newspapers and yearbooks. They're upstairs and they have it roped off."

I look where she's looking, and sure enough, there's a velvet rope draped across the staircase leading up. There's a sign that says DO NOT ENTER.

"You're going to let a sign stop us?" Samir asks. "Aren't we supposed to be delinquents?" And with that, he marches straight over to the staircase and steps right over the velvet rope.

Hana looks at me, and we both shrug and then follow Samir up the stairs.

Upstairs, the lights aren't on and it's darker and more musty smelling than downstairs. It's that old-attic smell, sort of like mothballs and Grandma's house. I'm not sure how we're supposed to find anything in the semidark. Samir leads us straight to the old school yearbooks.

"I thought you never went into the library," Hana says, amazed.

"I said I didn't study in the library," Samir says. "But I know where the yearbooks are. How do you think I do research on all the hot sophomores?"

"I thought you preferred freshmen," I say.

"That's this year," Samir says. "Sophomores were last year." He winks at me.

"Guess I missed my window then," I say. "That's too bad."

"I would definitely make an exception for you," Samir says.

"She was clearly kidding, you dork," Hana says. "Anyway, I'm going to go find the local newspaper stuff." Hana ducks down the next aisle.

I pull out the 1990 yearbook. I flip to the S's, finding Kate Shaw at the top corner of the page. She has dark, straight hair and good cheekbones, and carefully done makeup. In a word, pretty.

I take a closer look.

Actually, she looks a lot like . . . well, *me*.

I feel something cold in the pit of my stomach. This is not the kind of coincidence I was prepared for.

"Whoa, she was hot," Samir says. "How come that wasn't in the campus legend?" He grabs the yearbook from me and turns the picture around so he can see it better. "Actually, you know, she looks an awful lot like . . ."

"Don't say it," I say.

"You," he finishes. "Wow, that's kind of weird."

"Tell me about it."

We could practically be sisters.

I look at the picture again. She is smiling, which is weird because very few of her classmates are. The yearbook as a whole has a feeling of mug shots from prison. But Kate seems different. She seems perky, even *happy,* which is weird considering she was sent here. But then I think back to her signature with the heart.

I flip through other parts of the yearbook, but find no more pictures of Kate. "I wonder what Ms. W looked like fifteen years ago," I ask. "Or Headmaster B! That I would pay to see. You think they were here then?"

I flip through, but there are no pictures of faculty. None. Not even standing around in the background of a campus shot.

"No teachers—that's weird," I say.

"What's weird is that a place like Bard has yearbooks at all. Can you imagine wanting anybody here to sign it?"

Samir has a point.

"Found it," Hana says, carrying an old bound volume of newspaper clippings. It's a local town newspaper, called the Maine Township *Globe.* Hana has it open to an issue dated November 5, 1990. The headline reads "Student Still Missing."

"You know what's weird," Hana adds, "this girl looks like . . ."

"Miranda? Yeah, we know already," Samir says, showing Hana the yearbook.

While the two of them draw similarities, I start to read the newspaper article:

> Kate Shaw, a sophomore at the local boarding school Bard Academy, is still missing and police fear the worst. Shaw, 15, disappeared from her room Halloween night and police have called for an intensive search of the area. Her backpack was found in the woods near the campus three days ago, and police say traces of blood on the backpack point to foul play.

"Wow, the story *is* real," Samir says, whistling. "I wonder what other campus legends are true. Maybe this means it's true that Bard is a secret psychology experiment. Or that the cafeteria gravy is actually made from dead students."

"Wait, does this say she went missing on Halloween?" I ask, rereading the story. "That's the date that's carved into my closet floor. It's October 31, 1990." I reread the story and something strikes me as odd. "They don't mention her family at all. No parents or siblings or anything."

"Weird," Hana says, shifting the big book in her arms. As she does so, a small, thin book slides out of the bound volume.

"Hey, what's this?" Samir asks, stooping to pick it up. It's an old book, with tiny gold print on the outside.

It says "Bard Academy for Boys, 1855." Inside, there's a large picture of an old class.

It is a yearbook, but not like any I've seen. There's just one picture in it, and a lot of typed words, spelling out the school's classes and facilities. I suppose it's less like a yearbook and more like a publicity brochure, circa 1855.

The one picture shows some students standing in front of the old chapel. It looks exactly the same, even though the students are dressed in old-fashioned clothes. The boys are wearing knickers and newsboy caps. It's just one photo, the students in rows, and sitting in chairs, with the teachers standing behind them. It's grainy and old, but definitely a photograph.

"Wow, read this," Hana says, of the paragraph at the bottom of the page.

"Does it say the academy was built on an ancient Indian burial ground?" Samir asks.

"Not exactly. But the school was built on top of an old colonial school that burned to the ground in 1847. Thirty students died in that fire. The chapel is new in this picture, see? Built in 1855."

"I think that counts as being built on graves," Samir says. "Even if they aren't Indian. That's another true campus legend."

There's a woman standing beside another teacher, and someone has circled her head in pencil. She's clearly a teacher, but her face is a bit blurred, like she just moved at the last second. It's an old photograph, and those old cameras didn't do well with movement. But oddly enough, all the teachers are like that. Each of their faces is blurred, even though all the students' faces are mostly clear.

Out of curiosity, I flip to the back to see who's checked it out. That's when I see Kate Shaw's name, right on the last line. She was the last person to have this book, and it's stamped October 1990, the very month she disappeared. That's a strange coincidence. Who put this book in with the newspaper clippings of Kate's disappearance? Strange.

"Well, I'm taking this with us," I say of the slim Bard Academy yearbook. "I think it has something to do with Kate Shaw's disappearance."

"Who are you? Veronica Mars?" Samir asks me.

"Look, I'm the one who's living with Kate's ghost, or whatever," I say, noting the skepticism on their faces. And granted, a hall light isn't a ghost, but it sort of feels like one. If it's not her ghost, then it's a weird co-incidence that she seems to be pointing me in the direction of clues. "At least I can try to figure out what happened. Besides, if I can prove that this school is unsafe, then I get a one-way ticket home."

"Come on, let's go get our schedules for Neptune High," Samir says, as he starts to hum Elvis Costello's "Veronica."

Ten

My schedule reads like some kind of insane *Amazing Race* itinerary. Every little bit of time from the moment I get up (6:30 A.M.) until I go to sleep (10:00 P.M.) is marked by some activity. If it's not class, it's counseling or study time, and if it's not that, it's mandatory extracurricular activities, like yearbook or school newspaper or sports.

"Basketball?" I cry, looking at my schedule. It's marked there every afternoon from four to six. "I can't play basketball. I've never played in my whole life."

I've had a doctor's note to get out of every gym class since I started middle school. These came courtesy of my friend Liz, whose dad is a doctor, a podiatrist, but he's got really cool stationery that says "From the Desk of Dr. Pauley." Liz makes up a new ailment every year to get out of gym class herself, but I stick to the tried and true: asthma (which, by the way, is a total lie).

"Sports are mandatory," Samir tells me. "We all have them. And most of them are coached by Coach H."

"Wait? The guy who wears the baseball cap? The alcoholic?"

"Yep—that's the guy."

"Don't talk back to him. He likes to make you run laps," Hana says, looking like she knows about this firsthand.

I can't help but wonder if this is my dad's doing. He's always telling me about the power of sports, and trying to get me to try out for them. He doesn't realize that the only contact sport I'm interested in is fighting the crowds at the outlet mall.

"I wonder what sport Kate Shaw had to play," Hana says.

"Probably Track and Field," Samir says. "You know, since she did try to run away."

"Bad taste, Samir," Hana says.

"What? I'm just saying," Samir adds.

"I wonder if I sent a copy of the newspaper article to my parents if they'd come and get me?" I ask. "The sort of place where fifteen-year-olds disappear probably isn't the safest."

"Only if your parents care," Hana adds. "Mine don't. They wouldn't care if I was being taught by Saddam Hussein as long as I was out of their hair."

"You're lucky," Samir says. "My parents care *too* much about me, which is why they want me to marry a girl who's four feet tall and who I've known since I was six. I'd take parental neglect any day, thank you."

"Well, lucky for us, we have mandatory counseling sessions," Hana says, pointing to our schedules. "And looks like you're first, Miranda."

My counseling session happens that afternoon, after we've run through half the Sunday schedule (including breakfast, the nondenominational chapel service, lunch, and a trip to the bookstore to get our books for class). Honestly, I'm surprised they don't just write in mandatory pee breaks. This place is more regulated than boot camp.

My assigned counseling session happens in Ms. W's room at Capulet dorm.

"So your parents got divorced," she says to me, as we sit in her room, a small, studylike space. I notice that there's no bed visible. I wonder if this is why there's a campus legend about the teachers around here never needing sleep. There's just a desk, a love seat, and a couple of chairs. "How did that make you feel?"

"I don't know. How do you think I feel?" I say.

I like Ms. W, but this sounds like a really dumb question to me. Ms. W doesn't say anything. She just looks at me.

"Dad is a jerk, and Mom is a wreck. And it's five years later," I say.

"I've read your file. Why do you think you wrecked your dad's car?"

"Because a tree got in my way," I quip. This is, technically, true.

"Miranda, what's the real reason?" Ms. W sounds like she's starting to get annoyed.

"I was just picking up my sister, you know. She had this bully problem."

"Why couldn't your dad help your sister?"

"Please. He doesn't even know our middle names."

"And your mother? Where was she?"

I shrug.

"Does that happen a lot? Do you have to look after your sister because your parents don't?"

"I dunno. I guess."

I do feel like I'm the only one who seems to understand what's going on with Lindsay, or really, with anything else. I'm the one who cooks dinner mostly (Mom can't boil water, and if I don't cook something then it's order takeout). Dad's MIA. At least half the weekends Lindsay and I are supposed to see him, Dad has Carmen take us and do something like shopping while he hits the golf course. His excuse is that we'd rather do "girly" things. I don't call watching my stepmom snap at clerks at Saks Fifth Avenue girly. Neither is watching my college fund go down the drain.

"And if you're taking care of your sister and your mom, and your dad is missing in action, then who's taking care of you?" Ms. W asks me. "Did you ever think that maybe they're the ones who are supposed to take care of you?"

I shrug.

"Can you see that maybe you were acting out to

prove to them, and maybe yourself, that you *are* the kid. Not the adult."

I think about this. Maybe she's right. Maybe wrecking Dad's car, charging up Carmen's credit cards, and then going out with a known date rapist was my way of acting out. My way of saying, "Hey! I'm the kid— remember? You're supposed to take care of me!"

Ms. W tells me I should think about writing out my feelings to both parents in a letter. My "assignment" for counseling is to have a letter written in a month.

"Anything else bothering you?" she asks me, before I go.

I pause a second. "Well, there is this other thing," I say. I'm not sure how to tell her I think my dorm room might be haunted by Kate Shaw.

"Have you heard of Kate Shaw?" I ask her.

Ms. W looks startled, and then manages to put her features into a neutral expression. "Hers is a very sad story. How did you hear about her?"

"There are just rumors about her. The students talk about her. Did you know her? Were you here when she disappeared?"

"I was, yes, and I did know her. She lived in this dorm," Ms. W says. "She was a very bright girl. But she had terrible taste in boys, you know. She went for the disreputable ones, and I think that may have had something to do with why she disappeared."

"Really?"

"It just goes to show that you should be careful with

who you date," Ms. W says, looking at me as if she's trying to give me some advice.

"Do you think I look like her? Like Kate?"

Ms. W looks down at the notepad on her lap. "I think maybe this place can make you see things that aren't there. We're isolated, and the campus is old, and it's a fertile ground for ghost stories."

"I suppose, but—this is going to sound crazy—but I think her ghost is here. You know, in this dorm."

"I wouldn't worry about ghosts," Ms. W says. "I mean, do *I* look like a ghost to you?"

I look at her and giggle a little.

"No," I say.

"Then you have nothing whatsoever to worry about," she says, and gives me a small smile. "Because I'm the scariest thing you'll find here."

Eleven

"So Ms. W *knew* Kate? That is whacked," Samir says at dinner. I'm sitting with him and Hana and I've filled them in on the session with Ms. W.

"She thinks some stalker boyfriend killed her," I say.

"That's really sad," Hana adds.

"Maybe that's just something Ms. W says to girls so they don't date," Samir says. "Maybe she's an abstinence freak."

"There's nothing wrong with abstinence, you perv," Hana says.

"Sure, if it's voluntary," Samir says. "Mine is forced."

"Ignore him," Hana tells me. "He's just mad because his counselor—Mr. F—made him do 'the chair' today."

"What's that?"

"It's when you sit and talk to an empty chair and pretend it's whoever is really messing up your life at the moment," Hana says. "And Samir had to spend an hour talking to an empty chair and pretending it was his mom."

"At least I didn't pull a Parker Rodham," Samir says. "She got so mad she actually split the chair in half."

"Seriously?"

"The girl tried to kill her mom, remember? She has more issues than *Vogue*," Hana says.

I'm thinking about this when I look up and see Ryan Kent. He's just finished dinner and he's headed right for me.

I freeze, fork halfway to my mouth. It dawns on me that with my haste to go find Samir and Hana this morning, I ran out of my room without makeup or a single accessory. I'm not even sure if I remembered to comb my hair. This is so not the first impression I need to make on the hottest guy in class.

Then again, he probably doesn't even remember me. We had yearbook together last year. I took the opportunity to stake out the territory of platonic friendship. I knew I could never be girlfriend material (Ryan typically rotates through the school's most *YM* cover-ready girls, almost all of them with two-syllable names ending in "y"—like Britney, Jenny, Mandy), so I decided to go for the friends-only approach.

Ryan seemed to appreciate the fact that I didn't drool over him, like some girls, or stutter when he came into the room. You should see his effect on most girls. It's like instant lobotomy. Not that I don't find him attractive. I do. But I'm not about to lose my crap just because he has washboard abs. (Yes, I've seen them on that rare occasion when he takes off his basketball shirt on the bench and changes into a new one. I'm not blind.)

"Oh my God—Miranda, is that you?" Ryan says, his face breaking out into a smile that deserves to be on the cover of an Abercrombie catalog.

"Ryan," I sputter, not sure what to say. Am I supposed to acknowledge the fact that he was in a car accident that killed his girlfriend (he passed an alcohol test, but word was he was still at fault)? Or do I just pretend like nothing happened?

"God, it's good to see a friendly face," he says, and he hugs me. No kidding. *Hugs* me. Puts his beefy triceps around me and squeezes.

Next to me, Hana goes stock-still and loses her ability to form words. I'm sure she, like every other girl in this school, has a minor crush on Ryan. Honestly, you don't even really have to have a crush on Ryan to go all to goo in front of him. Just two X chromosomes and a pulse, really. But I'm not going to melt into a puddle. He's just a boy. Even if he is a really good-looking one.

Samir, for his part, ignores Ryan altogether, and focuses hard on his own pancakes.

"What's up with those shoes?" I ask him, looking at his feet so as not to become distracted by his very fit arms, chest, and stomach. He's wearing Converse low-tops, which are flawless except for one scuff mark on the right toe.

"What's wrong with my shoes?" Ryan asks me.

"I think I can see your big toe."

"Cannot," he says, giving my arm a playful push. "They're comfy. I like them."

I can't help but tease him. He's so tease-able, in large part because no one ever dares to make fun of him. But teasing him helps me remind myself he's just human, and not Heath Ledger's long-lost twin. If I didn't, then I'd turn into an ice statue like Hana sitting next to me. She practically has her fork frozen in the air on the way to her mouth. She's about to start drooling.

"They're three steps away from being sandals," I tease.

"Nice try, Ms. Fashion Police, but these have a few miles in them yet," he says, still smiling. He always takes my ribbing in good fun. After all, I'm the only girl in school who ever dared tell him he's not drop-dead gorgeous. Honestly, he probably likes to hear something different now and again. I like to think I'm doing my part to prevent his ego from spiraling out of control. One day, he'll thank me. And, hopefully, confess his undying love while he's at it.

"So why are you here? Are you going to give everybody a makeover? I have a feeling you have your work cut out for you."

"I wish. I wrecked my dad's car," I say. "But if I would've known he'd send me here, I would've done something really bad, like break his new golf clubs."

Ryan barks a laugh. His grin gets bigger.

"Well, really good to see you. I guess I'll see you around then," he says, and smiles.

"Yeah, uh, definitely," I say a little too eagerly.

I watch as Ryan and his perfectly toned butt walk away from us. Hana, who has been frozen in lust or shock, I can't tell which, gurgles to life next to me.

"He's so c-c-c-cute," Hana stammers. She's still somewhat under the influence of Ryan. Like alcohol, he can make you slur your speech. "I don't know how you can actually carry on a conversation with him."

"He's not so great," Samir grumbles.

"It's mind over hormones. Mind over hormones." I pause, letting out the breath I'd semi-been holding since first seeing Ryan. "Besides, he's not my type anyway."

"Not your type! Only if you're dead," she says. "Uh-oh, don't look now, but Ryan isn't the only one giving you some attention."

I follow Hana's eyes and see that at a neighboring table, Parker Rodham, the Queen Bee, is glaring at me. I can feel the hostility rolling off her in waves. Both she and her posse are staring at me. If they had laser vision, I'd be a Pop-Tart by now.

"I think that's a new record," Hana says. "Fastest time someone has made an enemy of Parker Rodham."

"My mom always says I'm good at making new friends," I say, beginning to wish that I was back to just dealing with ghosts.

Twelve

Back in my room, my window is miraculously fixed, although there's no explanation for it. Blade said she didn't see any workers come in to replace the windowpane, but there it is, brand new. I would've thought I'd imagined the whole thing, except that Blade saw it, too.

That evening, I drift into another fitful night of sleep. Cue ghost-floating-outside-my-window nightmare. I'm beginning to think that the ghost in my dream is Kate Shaw, since she does look like me. This doesn't change the fact that it is still scary, and I wake up feeling like I didn't really sleep at all. Even worse, after I get up, I discover I have an even bigger problem than no sleep. Namely, a zit the size of a Hummer.

I could've predicted it.

This always happens to me on the first day of school, without fail. I have to have some mortifying skin problem just because the first day of school isn't hard enough all on its own.

The thing is, it's all about timing. It's not like I have breakouts all the time. Just at key moments. When I'm on vacation with Lindsay and Mom where no one sees me and I spend the entire time in yoga pants with my hair in a ponytail—well, I have flawless skin. Not a breakout in sight. But give me a date, a dance, or an oral report and it's like a lost ridge of the Rocky Mountains decides to erupt on my face. That's because the Clearasil gods hate me.

When emergency concealer doesn't work, I hide my face with a newsboy cap. When biology fails you, you can always count on ingenuity.

I've fooled around too long. I've already missed breakfast and if I don't hurry, I'm going to miss morning assembly, too.

Morning assembly (which is sort of like morning announcements) is directed by Headmaster B, and held every morning before class at the campus chapel. This is the first day of classes, and the first morning assembly, but according to Samir and Hana it's more important to be on time for this than for your own class. Headmaster B doesn't tolerate tardiness, and the last student to assembly on the first day of class spent the first week cleaning dishes every night and every morning.

I have less than a minute to get across campus, and

even if I sprint, I doubt I'm going to make it. As I think I've mentioned before, I am not what you'd call especially athletic. My idea of exercise is to flip through *Teen Vogue.*

I burst through the chapel doors only to find everyone is inside, and Headmaster B standing at the podium. All eyes turn toward me as the bangles on my arm clink together, making a sound louder than the chapel bell.

Um, can you say "embarrassing"?

I feel my face flush red, and naturally, that's the moment when I look up and see Ryan Kent staring at me, a puzzled look on his face. Then there's Hana and Samir two rows down from him, giving me pitying looks. Ms. W just shakes her head and puts her head in her hands, disappointed.

"Sorry," I say, holding up a hand, which sends another loud clank of metal-on-metal bracelets together. I slide into the last row of seats and stumble a little, sitting down hard on my butt on one of them, my bracelets clanging like an annoyingly loud ringtone. Note to self: get quieter accessories.

I tug on my newsboy cap, wishing I'd bought one big enough to fit my whole body in.

"Ms. Tate," Headmaster B says, sounding particularly annoyed. "Congratulations. You are the last student to assembly, and you'll be the first this semester to enjoy dish duty at Bard Academy."

There are snickers, and everyone is still staring at me. This is so embarrassing. It's one of those times I wished they made an emergency jet pack. They could keep it in high school buildings around the country in glass cases right next to fire extinguishers, except that on the outside of the cabinet it would say "In Cases of Extreme Humiliation, Break Glass."

Barring that jet pack, I think I am pretty much stuck being the center of attention at the moment. Parker Rodham and her clones point at me and whisper to themselves something that makes them all laugh.

"You shall report to the cafeteria . . ." Headmaster B is interrupted by the chapel door, which swings open and bounces against the wall.

Heathcliff walks in, or I should say *strolls,* because he certainly doesn't look like he is in a hurry to get anywhere. His black eye has faded, and he's wearing his Bard Academy uniform with the top button open and the tie loose. He stares at Headmaster B, and then at all the faculty members sitting at the front of the chapel, as if daring them to do something to him.

I've never been so glad to see him. He's just gotten me out of dish duty.

He glances over at me, giving a slight nod in my direction. I can't help but feel that he did this on purpose somehow. That he's saved me.

The faculty members look a bit flustered, because they start talking among themselves, and even Headmaster B is temporarily speechless. I get the feeling there's something else going on here that I don't know about.

And then, as everyone watches, Heathcliff turns around and leaves, swinging the chapel door wide behind him. I have to hand it to him. He has moxie.

Two Guardians head after him out the door.

All the kids start whispering and murmuring. In that one instant, he just became the school hero, I think. Still, chances are he'll spend the rest of the semester in solitary confinement as soon as the Guardians catch up to him.

"That's enough, students," Headmaster B says, slapping a ruler hard against the podium. "Enough entertainment for one morning, I should think. Let us focus on the task at hand. And Ms. Tate, I expect you to pay attention, especially now that your friend has gotten you out of your punishment. That is, unless you'd rather just do the dishes for fun?"

"No, Headmaster," I say, feeling everyone's eyes on me again. And I know it's just going to be one of those days.

You know the kind of day when you simply can't do anything right? If there really were Humiliation Escape jet packs, I would've used every last one on campus. Let's recap:

1) Morning assembly debacle
2) Couldn't find a single class on campus, when everyone else seems to have no problems at all.
3) Walked into one of Ryan Kent's classes by mis-

take, only to be told by his teacher that I was in the wrong building.

4) During history class, when Coach H called on me, I had been reading one of the Bard yearbooks and didn't realize he was talking about Franz Ferdinand *the archduke of Spain whose assassination set off World War I,* and not Franz Ferdinand the band.

5) Was so tired from not sleeping most of the night that I fell asleep in English lit, right after our teacher, Ms. P, passed out our reading assignment (*Wuthering Heights*—again, big surprise—I can't get away from that book), and woke up in a puddle of my own drool. One of Parker's clones pointed and laughed at me, and then passed me a note that said, "You were snoring."

6) A girl faints in the hall (she was probably anorexic), and Blade insists it was because she'd been bitten by a vampire. In fact, shouts it for everyone to hear, with me standing right next to her, and then says, "My roommate will tell you— it's true!" Because my social life isn't enough of a vacuum at this point. I really wish she'd go back to her vow of silence.

7) At basketball practice, I'm so inept, that I can't even dribble the ball. I keep hitting it off my foot, sending it rolling off onto the next court (the boy's), where Ryan Kent is. He even witnesses my ball-in-the-face, when I don't realize another

girl is passing to me and she hits me in the side of the head. *Ka-pow.* Coach H then makes me run five laps around the gym.

By dinnertime, I am so sore (both physically and mentally) that I don't even care what the food is on our plates (hot dogs—something semirecognizable). Hana and Samir and Ryan Kent are MIA, and even Blade isn't anywhere to be found. I'm once again alone in the cafeteria. If I have to sit by myself, I swear I'm going to sue my parents later for emotional scarring. I had plenty of friends at my old school. I never, under almost any circumstances, ate alone there. It's like my dad is trying to undermine my self-esteem. As if he didn't accomplish that enough by ignoring me.

That's when I look up and see Heathcliff.

He's sitting by himself in the corner, staring at the hot dog on his plate as if he's never seen one before. He picks up the hot dog and examines it, and then sniffs at it. It looks like he can't decide whether or not it's edible. I know how he feels.

"That was some trick you pulled this morning," I say, as I put my tray down in front of him. Instantly, he stands up and gives me a little bow. Is this some kind of British chivalry? I don't know.

"Is it okay if I sit here?" I ask, still not sure what he's doing standing up.

He nods at me, but says nothing. I sit, and then he sits.

"Did you get in trouble?" I ask him. He looks up at me, reluctantly almost, and shrugs. "I should probably thank you, you know. You saved me a lot of dish washing."

"Washing dishes is beneath you," he says. I wonder for a moment if he's being sarcastic, but I see that he's serious. He means it. He thinks I shouldn't wash dishes—ever. That's some serious chivalry.

"So why are you here?" I ask him. "What did you do to get sent away?"

He shrugs.

"You don't say much, do you?"

He shrugs again.

"In a conversation, when I ask a question, you're supposed to answer," I tease him. "That's how conversations work. And then you can ask me a question, and I answer. Like, you can say, 'Wow, the food is really bad here, don't you think?' and then I say, 'Oh yeah, it's terrible. What classes do you have?' and so on."

He just looks at me, the half scowl he usually wears on his face replaced by something that looks a little more like confusion. I can see he's not the talkative type.

"Okay, I'll start the conversation. My parents suck, which is why I'm here," I say, figuring this might be a safe line of conversation. Nearly every kid in this place has a beef with one parent or both. "What about yours?"

"My parents are dead," he says.

Instantly, I feel like an idiot. "Oh my God, I'm sorry," I say.

He shrugs. "I never really knew them," he says. "I was taken in by a man and his family."

"In a place called Wuthering Heights?"

He nods.

"Is that in England?" I ask, trying to place his accent.

He nods again.

"Well, I told you there was a book by that same name," I say, reaching into my backpack and showing him my paperback copy of *Wuthering Heights* from English lit. "And you know there's a Heathcliff in it, too."

I heard that much about the book, at least, before I fell asleep in class.

Heathcliff looks surprised.

"That's some coincidence, isn't it?" I ask him. "But I guess you don't read much?"

He takes the book from my hand and studies it, a questioning look on his face. He turns the book upside down and then opens it up. It occurs to me quite suddenly that it's not that he doesn't read, but that *he can't read*. I take the book from him and put it the right way.

"You can't read, can you?" I ask him.

He drops the book, looks down at his tray, and then turns his attention back to his hot dog, which he picks up and nearly eats in one bite. I think I've embarrassed him. I feel bad about it, because the last thing I want to do is make him feel stupid. First, I bring up painful memories about his dead parents, and now I point out that he can't read. Wow, I am on a roll.

I can only imagine all the teasing he's gotten about

not being able to read. And there could be a million different reasons he didn't learn to read. Maybe he has dyslexia.

"You know, I could teach you," I say, without thinking it through. First, I have no idea how to teach someone to read, and second, do I really want a lot of one-on-one time with what could be the biggest troublemaker in school? Still, I brush those thoughts aside. I owe him, and if he needs tutoring help, then so be it. And besides, don't I pride myself on being friends with everybody? I don't make snap judgments about people. Not like the Parker Rodhams of the world. The last thing I am is a snob.

Heathcliff looks up at me and there's hope on his face, and maybe even the trace of a smile. He seems to like the idea. But just as suddenly as the cloud lifted from his face, it descends again and his lip curls into a scowl. His eyes are focused on something beyond my left shoulder and when I turn to see what he's looking at, I see two Guardians headed our way from across the cafeteria. They seem to be after Heathcliff. In fact, they have their police batons out, as if they anticipate a fight.

"Uh-oh. It looks like you might be in some trouble. What did you do now?" I ask, turning back around. But I discover that I'm talking to an empty chair. Heathcliff has gone. All that's left is his tray with his half-eaten hot dog. I scan the cafeteria, but see no trace of him. I look under the table, but he's not there, either. He disappeared.

"Where did he go?" a Guardian asks me gruffly.

"I don't know," I say.

The Guardians push past me, into the crowd of students by the dish-washing station, but they've lost him, too. Secretly, I find myself glad he got away.

Thirteen

After dinner, I head to the bathroom for mandatory shower time. I'm late for my shower, on purpose, because this means I'll miss most of the other girls. I don't need everyone to see me naked, thanks.

I'm so sore from basketball and running around campus that all I want to do is have a long soak in the shower. Unfortunately, there's nothing about our dorm bathrooms that is relaxing or soothing. It's kind of like taking a bath in the public bathroom at the airport. You know that everything is filthy.

The worst part is that I didn't bring flip-flops, and the tile floor is disgusting. The bathroom is dark and dank, like nearly every other place at Bard Academy. It's got black-and-white tiles on the floor, and the toilets in the stalls have *wooden* toilet seats. The toilets also have those weird, high backs, with long chains for flushing. Porta-Potties have more amenities.

The showers are in the back, white stalls (well, more like once were white, but now sludge gray color with soap scum and mildew). They're empty, as usual. No one likes to use them. I saw a girl washing out her armpits in the sink yesterday.

I take the first stall on the left and turn on the hot water. Okay. Commence Fastest Shower in the History of Mankind. I run through the shampoo and skip the second round and the conditioner. I'm rinsing out Pantene, when I hear the sound of . . . laughter. It's faint at first and then it grows louder. It's not the happy kind. It's the creepy I'm-a-crazed-killer kind.

Okay. I'm naked. In a mildew-infested shower. The possibilities of foot fungus are scary enough. I don't need any enhancements here, people.

"Who is that?" I call, hoping the peevish sound of my voice discourages whatever delinquent prankster thought it would be a good idea to hit me when I was most vulnerable.

"Is someone in here?" My voice echoes in the bathroom. Naturally, they don't answer. The sound of laughter gets louder. It's hard to tell where the sound is coming from, but I can definitely tell that it's a girl's voice, not a boy's. It's a girl or woman, and she's laughing her demonically possessed head off.

"Okay, whoever is doing that, it's not funny," I say, trying on my best I'm-not-really-freaked-out-by-the-weird-maniacal-laughter voice. I finish rinsing and then turn off the shower. I'm in the process of throwing on my pajamas, even though I'm still wet. While I'm yanking on my shirt, the lights go out.

The hairs on my forearm stand up. Okay, forget trying to be cool. I'm outta here. I jump into my Pumas, feet still wet, and scramble out of the shower stall, my pajamas sticking to me in odd places, as I feel my way along the tiled wall toward the door. I'm groping my way along the wall, hoping to find the light switch. I make it five steps, then six, but instead of feeling a switch, my hand suddenly touches another hand.

"Ack," I cry, recoiling. "Who's there? Who is that?"

No one answers me. I put a foot out in front of me, but no one is there. Tentatively, I put my hand back on the wall, but I just feel the cool, smooth tile. Stay calm, I tell myself, and just get to the door.

My hand falls on the door and I push it open and stumble out of the bathroom. Outside, I smell smoke. Something is burning. At the end of the hall, I see Hana turning the corner. Before I can call out, I realize that the smoke in the hall is coming from my room.

I rush in, pushing open the door. There's no sign of Blade, but there is a fire burning brightly in our trashcan. Without thinking, I stomp on it, trying to put it out, and in the process semiruin my favorite pair of Pumas.

Could this be Kate's doing? Did her ghost set this fire?

"Hey!" cries Blade, appearing at the door. Ms. W appears right behind her, frowning.

"Are you all right, Miranda?" Ms. W asks, worried.

"I'm okay," I say, feeling glad that somebody around here cares if I live or die.

"I'm fine, if you consider that my roommate just tried to burn down the dorm," Blade says.

"Me? I didn't do this," I exclaim. "It had to be you."

"Wasn't me. I was in the den," Blade says.

"Now, Miranda. I thought we talked about this."

I suppose she's referring to the acting-bad-as-a-way-to-get-attention talk during our session.

"But I didn't do this—I swear!" I hate that she thinks I'm responsible for this. "I understand that acting out isn't going to get me the kind of attention I want. And look, all I want to do is go home. Setting a fire isn't going to do that."

I try to show that I'm logical. I'm reasonable. Still, Ms. W looks at me with some doubt on her face. Blade looks at me, too.

"It could always be the vampire," she says. "He's definitely a troublemaker."

I smack my palm against my head. Vampires! First, my room has a ghost, then a pyromaniac starts a fire in my trashcan, and now my roommate's going on about her vampire obsession. It has got to stop.

"I told her to wear garlic," Blade tells Ms. W, "but she won't listen to me."

"That's nice," Ms. W says, clearly not believing Blade. "As for you," she says, looking at me, "I *will* send you to the headmaster's office if I so much as even see a match in this room, you understand?"

I nod. "Yes, Ms. W."

"Good. Now both of you—to bed."

"But it's only nine," Blade whines.

"To *bed,*" Ms. W says in a tone that doesn't leave open room for argument.

That night, I have the same nightmare—again—and wake up even before the bugle. It's the same, in fact, for the next five nights in a row. My Worst Day Ever turns into my Worst Week Ever; between my nightmares and not getting any sleep, I am even more of a zombie than I was the first day of classes. I keep showing up late, and getting lost, and pretty much making a fool out of myself at every available opportunity. I still don't know who started the fire, and Hana says she didn't see anything.

I don't know why, but I think the fire, Kate Shaw, and my nightmares might be connected somehow, but I don't know how. In my (very little) free time, I try to find out more about Kate. Oddly, in all the newspaper clippings, there's no mention of a family or siblings. It's like she didn't have any ties at all.

I also discover that she checked out other old yearbooks from the library, not just the 1855 one. She checked out almost all of them, at one time or another, but in particular, the ones she checked out the most were 1855, 1848, and 1849. She borrowed those four separate times, which means she had them out for two months apiece. And, in each one, it seems like she might have circled a picture of a faculty member. And each picture is too blurry to make out the teacher's face. I have three of them in my room, trying to make sense of what she was looking for. I'm not sure if it's even related to why she disappeared.

By the end of the week, I meet with Ms. W again and she asks me how my letter to my dad is coming. It's not, really. I've got a bunch of balled-up pieces of paper in my trashcan, but that's about it. I've had other things on my mind.

Besides, it's hard to write my dad, because I don't really know what to say to him. Although I can think of two words I wouldn't mind writing, but Ms. W said I should try not to be profane.

In the meantime, Ms. W gives me letters from Mom and Lindsay. They've both written me one for every day I've been here. Dad hasn't, though. I try to not be upset by it. I wonder why, when my expectations are so low, that he still manages to disappoint me.

I still want to get out of here, but in the meantime, I've decided to make the best of it. The teachers aren't as bad as I thought (Ms. P actually teaches a pretty mean sophomore lit class), and even though Coach H makes me run around the gym, he's an interesting history teacher. He brought actual World War I artifacts to class the other day, including a bullet he said was pulled from a soldier's leg. Now, try getting that kind of hands-on learning at my old public school. Fat chance.

After one week of classes, I find that I have more work than I did during a whole semester at my old school, which means that I have less time to worry about the mystery of Kate Shaw, why Heathcliff seems to be able to disappear into thin air, who set a fire in my room, and pretty much life in general that doesn't involve homework.

For two hours after dinner every night, we're supposed to study, read, write letters, or basically do anything constructive by yourself sitting at your desk. Your other choice is to just go to bed early, which is what Blade does, because she's piled into her bed at 8:00 P.M., and is snoring. I don't know how she can manage to sleep so soundly in this place—especially if she thinks vampires are about. But then again, she does have a poster of Satan above her bed, so she's clearly not like the rest of us.

I settle down to read *Wuthering Heights* for English lit. As I get into the book, I can't help but start thinking about some weird coincidences. Two things immediately strike me as strange. One, Heathcliff in the book is *a lot* like Heathcliff at Bard. They are both surly, tough, and adopted, and they are both semi-obsessed with a girl named Cathy.

Is Heathcliff obsessed with this book? Is he trying to *be* Heathcliff? But then again, he can't read, right? Unless he's faking that, too.

Another strange parallel is that a character in this book has the *exact same* nightmare I am having. The ghost outside the window, asking to be let in.

Very weird. It's like life imitating art, for real. I'm not

sure what to make of it. I look at the front of my book and see that it was originally published in 1847. That date sounds familiar for some reason. I look down at my backpack and see the Bard Academy 1855 Yearbook.

I open it, and sure enough, 1847 is the year that the original Bard Academy burned down.

That's some odd coincidence. Did Kate figure out some connection between the three? The fire and the publication of the two books? In the front of my copy of *Wuthering Heights*, there's a foreword that discusses the life of Emily Brontë and her sisters. It says Emily (author of *Wuthering Heights*) died in 1848 of tuberculosis. Anne (*Agnes Gray*) followed in 1849 of the same. And then Charlotte (*Jane Eyre*) died in 1855 of "exhaustion," whatever that is.

1855.

1849.

1848.

Those are the same years of the Bard yearbooks that Kate checked out.

I get them from under my bed and open them again to the pages where teachers are circled. In each of the three, she has circled a female faculty member. But each face is blurred and indistinct.

Those dates, and then three different women. Is she trying to say that the Brontë sisters *didn't* die? That they somehow faked their deaths and then wound up at Bard?

I absently kick my foot out, and my shin hits the

edge of a drawer that's out slightly. Ow. I shut the drawer closed with my foot, rub my shin, and then go back to reading.

I peer at the circled picture in the 1848 catalog, but it's just another blurred face. There's no telling if the picture is anything like the painted portrait on the back cover of my copy of *Wuthering Heights.*

I swing my foot out and it hits the drawer—again.

Okay, this time I am not imagining it. I *just* closed it. Now it's open again. Something weird is going on here. I look down at the drawer, wondering if it's broken, when, inside the drawer, I see familiar handwriting. Kate has etched her initials here, too.

I feel my blood run cold. Is this another haunted closet situation? I guess Kate Shaw isn't done with me yet.

I open the drawer. It's empty. I pull on the drawer and lift it up and out of its track, then inspect it. It seems okay—there's a little raised piece of wood on each side of it that fits into the groves of the old desk. It doesn't seem broken or warped or anything. No reason that it would just slip open on its own. I put the drawer down and look into the empty drawer space. I pull down the desk lamp for light and peer in. It's empty, except for something sticking out at the back of the drawer, hanging from the top. Is it tape?

I put down the lamp and reach into the back of the drawer. I can't seem to reach whatever it is, so I lean in farther so that I'm nearly up to my armpit, and that's when I feel a hand grab my wrist.

I whip my arm free, and the force of my pulling flings my body several feet back and into Blade's desk so hard that I knock off her skull candle, which falls straight into my lap, with its two black eye sockets staring up at me and its mouth grinning its lipless grin.

Aaaaaaaaaaaaaaaack.

"Dammit, Blade," I mutter under my breath, relieved that I am in one piece, and that the skull is made of wax and isn't real. As if it isn't enough that I'm living with a girl ghost, I have to have Ms. Halloween as a roommate, too. Why couldn't I get the girl who loves pink, stuffed Teddy bears? No. I had to get the freak who likes skulls. It's no wonder I'm seeing ghosts everywhere.

Blade snorts and rolls over, still asleep.

I am breathing hard, but I carefully put the skull candle back up on her desk and reach back over to right the lamp I knocked over. Okay. Let's try this again. It probably *wasn't* a creepy skeleton ghost hand (like I imagined in my mind) that grabbed my wrist. I probably just got it caught on something, right? Okay, right. But better safe than sorry.

"Kate," I whisper, in a low voice while I look around the room, "if that is you, please stop scaring me half to freaking death, because I am trying to *help* you, okay?"

The room is silent.

"Okay, I'm going to take that as an apology, all right? Now, let's start again. No more grabbing on the first date. I am not that kind of girl."

I put the desk lamp back in front of the drawer and

peer in. That's when I see that there's some kind of key partly taped to the top of the drawer. It's now hanging loose, dangling. Either my gyrations or the skeleton hand knocked it part of the way free.

"I'm putting my hand in here now, but don't take any liberties. Just chill out."

I reach in quickly, grab the key, and yank it free, unmolested.

"Thank you," I say to the room. I look at the key. It's an old, worn brass one that fits into my palm. It has no inscription on it. It's just a key. But to what?

The Bard bell tolls, signaling lights out. I slip the key into my backpack pocket and put the drawer back in its rightful place, then switch off our lights.

I'm just crawling into bed when Ms. W sticks her head in my door.

"Everything okay in here? No fires, I hope?" she asks me.

"No fires," I say. Normally, I wouldn't mind talking to Ms. W, but I'm a bit preoccupied. It seems like the more I find out about Kate Shaw, the more mysteries she presents to me. I don't know what the Brontë sisters have to do with Bard, or what the key has to do with anything.

"You sure everything's okay?" Ms. W asks me.

"You mean everything aside from being here?"

"Oh, I'm that bad, am I?" she says, but I can tell she's teasing. She turns to go, and then pauses at the door. "You know it's okay to be upset."

"Upset? Why?" Does she know about my haunted room?

"With your father. For sending you here," she says, as if it's obvious that's what I should be upset about.

"Oh, right. Yeah," I say. I've sort of forgotten about him for the time being.

"You know sometimes parents don't do things for the best reasons," she says. "But sometimes it works out anyway. You know that if you want to talk . . ."

"You're here," I finish.

"You're catching on," Ms. W says. She steps away from my door and moves on down the hall.

I look down at the floor where she'd been standing and notice there's a puddle there, along with wet footprints down the hall. Odd. Why does she always leave a trail? One of these days, I'm going to have to ask her.

Fourteen

"If I could only talk to Kate somehow, then maybe I could figure all this out," I tell Hana and Samir the next day during study hall. We're all sitting together in the library, where we're supposed to be studying, but we're talking about Kate Shaw, as usual. I ought to form the Kate Shaw Mystery Society, since that's practically our whole focus these days.

"Who's Kate Shaw?" asks Blade, stopping at our table with a stack of books.

"Nobody," I say. The last thing I want to do is spend any more time with Blade than necessary. She's already obsessed with vampires. I don't want to add to her delusions.

"She's a ghost," Samir says.

"A ghost? Oooh, I like ghosts," Blade says, sitting down practically in Samir's lap and pretending to be very interested in everything he has to say. Does Blade *like* Samir? "Hi, I'm Blade. Who are you?"

"Samir," he says.

"Oooh, I *love* that name," Blade oozes, and then wraps her finger around one of his black curls. Samir doesn't quite know what to do with himself. He's not usually the object of such a strong come-on. I'm not sure what Blade is up to, but I'm sure it has something to do with witchcraft. Maybe she needs hair from a man for a spell.

Samir, in fact, is so taken aback by Blade that he doesn't even remember to propose (his usual MO when talking to a girl for the first time). Hana notices. And she doesn't like it. She starts to shifts uncomfortably.

"So what about this ghost?"

"The best campus legend," Samir starts.

"She's just a Bard student who disappeared fifteen years ago, presumed dead," Hana says, sounding irritated. "She used to live in your room."

I try to wave Hana off, but it's too late.

"My room? Really? We've got a ghost? Miranda, why didn't you tell me we had a ghost?"

"I don't think I said 'ghost,' " I say.

"That's exactly what you—" Samir starts before I kick him under the table. "Ow! What did you do that for?"

The last thing I want is for Blade to be in the Kate Shaw Mystery Society. She's likely to make us rub paint on our faces and run naked through the woods to try to get in touch with the spiritual world. No thanks. I've smelled her incense.

"I thought I picked up on something strange in the room," Blade says. "I thought it was just you or the vampire, but I guess there might be some spiritual activity. How did she die?"

"We don't know," Samir says.

"Well, why don't we find out?"

"How?"

"Let's ask her."

"You can't really think this will work," I say to Blade in our room later that night.

She has concocted a Ouija board, using nothing but a piece of poster paper she's drawn on with permanent marker and a glass she stole from the cafeteria.

Blade, Hana, and Samir are all sitting cross-legged on the floor. Samir has snuck into the room through the window, and if he's caught we'll probably all get dish duty.

I watch as Blade lights her skull candle and turns out the lights in the room.

"Is that really necessary?" I ask her.

"We have to set the mood," she says. "Now, you sit down on the floor, across from Hana. We all have to sit and hold hands."

"Come on, it'll be fun," Samir says.

"Very unlikely," Hana says. She's not happy to be sitting here at all. I get the distinct impression that she might like Samir herself. She certainly doesn't like Blade showing him any attention. "You know this isn't going to work," she adds now. She's even more skeptical than I am.

I sit down and look at the board. Across the top there are all the letters of the alphabet. In the middle there are just three words written: "yes," "no," and "maybe."

"Come on, you naysayers," Blade says, sitting back down and grabbing Samir's hand first and then mine. Reluctantly, Hana grabs my hand and then Samir's.

"Everyone, close your eyes," Blade tells us.

Then Blade starts to chant some kind of gibberish. I peek and see that Samir has his eyes tightly closed. Hana, however, is looking straight at Blade, skepticism written all over her face. Hana glances over at me and mouths, *Can you believe this?*

When Blade has finished her chanting, she instructs us all to put one finger on the top of the glass. Each of us do this, and then she asks the room, "Are there any spirits here?"

At first, nothing happens. The glass is still. Samir doesn't seem to care because he seems to be looking down Blade's shirt.

"I don't think this is working," Hana says. "Big surprise."

Blade ignores her. She asks the room again. "Are there any spirits here?"

This time, the glass starts inching forward, ever so slowly from the edge of the paper, toward the middle.

"Samir!" Hana says. "You're doing that."

"I'm not! I swear, I'm not," he says.

The glass moves slowly toward the "yes," and then stops on top of it.

"Oh, friendly spirit, please spell out your first and last initials for us," Blade says.

Again, the glass moves. First to the K. And then to the S.

"You have to be moving it," Hana says to Blade.

Blade, however, ignores her.

"Did something happen to you at Bard Academy?" Blade asks.

The glass, again, moves to "yes."

The hairs on my arms stand up a little. I look at Samir, and he's starting to look a little uneasy. I don't think he's consciously moving the glass.

But Hana gives me a look that says she thinks it's all garbage. That Blade is leading us on.

"Do you know the vampire on campus?" Blade asks.

This completely breaks the tension-filled moment. Hana actually laughs. Samir seems a little relieved. I guess he's not so brave after all. If he had a freshman here, she'd probably be comforting him, not the other way around.

"Vampire? What kind of question is that?" Hana asks. I have to agree.

"She's obsessed," I tell Hana and Samir.

"I'm not obsessed. I saw one," she tells them.

"Enough about vampires, Buffy," I say. "Let's get back to Kate, okay? I'm going to ask the next question. Kate, what is the key for?"

"Key? What key?" Blade asks.

The glass starts to move again. It heads to G, then to R, and then to E, E, and N.

"Green? What does that mean?" Hana asks.

"Wait, it's still moving," Samir says.

The next letters it lands on are H, O, U, S, and E.

"Green house? What green house? There aren't any green houses around here."

"No, wait," says Samir. "I think she means the greenhouse. You know, the one on the far north side of campus. With the flowers."

The glass starts to move again. It lands on the word "yes."

"See? Told you," Samir says.

"I think this is all a hoax," Hana says. "I think Blade has rigged this whole thing."

"Fine, I'll take my hand off entirely," Blade says, and she lifts off her finger, leaving just Samir, Hana, and me with our fingers on the glass.

"Kate—one last question," I say. "What are you trying to tell me about the teachers in the yearbooks? Are they the Brontë sisters?"

I watch as the glass slides back to "yes."

"Did the Brontë sisters fake their deaths?"

This time, however, the glass moves to "no."

"You can't say I did that this time," Blade says to Hana.

"What are you trying to tell me?" I ask, less to the room and more to myself. The glass moves again across the poster board, scraping the paper a little as it goes. It spells:

> THEY
> ARE
> DEAD

I get goose bumps on my arms.

"Stop it, Samir," Hana says, her voice a little panicked. She's a little bit uneasy now.

"I told you, I'm not doing it," Samir says, and then he pulls his finger away.

The glass, however, keeps moving.

It spells:

> DEAD
> DE

And then Hana pulls her finger away. "Okay, this isn't funny anymore," she says. I'm a bit freaked out myself and I pull my finger off, too.

But, as the four of us watch, the glass doesn't stop moving. It keeps spelling out the word. Then suddenly some force takes the glass and whips it off the board and across the room, breaking it into a dozen pieces against the wall.

That's when the lights in the room come on and we see Ms. W standing at the door.

"You four have some explaining to do," she says sternly. "And you'll be doing it in the headmaster's office."

Fifteen

Guardians escort the four of us to Headmaster B's office.

The Guardians don't speak to us, but just stare blankly ahead. There are four of them, as well, and they're wearing the Bard Guardian uniform, which is strikingly similar to the uniform worn by mall security. It's navy blue, and they've got baseball caps with the Bard crest on them.

By now, the campus is dark and the streetlamps are on, casting an eerie glow over everything.

I consider trying to run for it, but I know that the Guardians are quicker than they look. This morning I saw one tackle a kid who was trying to make off with a serving spoon from the dining room. I don't know what he was going to do with it, and probably the Guardians didn't, either, but he didn't make it very far before he was splayed on the ground with his hands behind his back. Blade looks resolute, Samir looks scared, and Hana looks annoyed.

The Guardians take us inside the office, where there's a fireplace and a giant mahogany desk, but no Headmaster B. We're told to sit in the four chairs facing Headmaster B's desk, as if she'd been expecting us already.

The Guardians draw back to the door of the room.

"This is all your fault," Hana whispers to Blade.

"No, this is *your* fault. Your skepticism angered that spirit," Blade says.

"There's no rule against séances, but there is one against having a boy in your room; ergo, ladies, it's my fault for sneaking into the room in the first place," Samir says, gallantly trying to take the blame.

"Shut up," both Blade and Hana say at the same time. Samir obliges.

A cold draft suddenly seeps into the room and I shiver.

"Miranda from *The Tempest*," Headmaster B says behind me, causing me to whip around. She is stealth. "I am very sorry to see you in my office so soon." Headmaster B takes a seat behind her desk as if nothing is amiss. She's so tiny that she looks a little like she's a child playing in her father's study.

She looks at each of us in turn.

"Now, Miranda, I understand that you and your friends have taken an acute interest in the disappearance of Kate Shaw. And that you were . . ." Headmaster B pauses and looks up as if trying to find the right word, ". . . trying to summon her with a séance. Is this right?"

Of course, when she says it, it sounds ridiculous.

"Yes," I say.

"And, were you successful in communicating with Kate Shaw?"

I'm thrown a bit by that question.

"Um, I think so, although we weren't sure."

"And what did she tell you?"

Again, I'm a bit surprised. Why is she showing such an interest in the séance? Shouldn't she be lecturing us on how we're being superstitious and unscientific, and it goes against the grain of academic excellence at a place like Bard? Instead, she seems to be taking the séance thing very seriously.

"She didn't tell us anything," Hana says, suddenly. "She told us the Brontë sisters were dead. Big deal. Everybody knows that."

I glance over at Hana. I'm not even sure that's what the ghost was trying to say. Or even if it was Kate we were talking to.

"I see," Headmaster B says, looking down at her hands, then folding them together on her desk. "Anything else?"

"She told us something happened to her here," Blade volunteers.

"You did that," Hana snipes. "It wasn't any ghost. And for all we know, you were the one who told us the Brontë sisters were dead, too."

"How could I? I wasn't even touching the glass then," Blade shouts.

"Children!" shouts Headmaster B. "Enough."

Everyone falls silent again. She considers us all in turn, as if trying to decide what to say to us.

"I strongly suggest that each one of you take a hard look at your behavior tonight and see where it has gotten you. The four of you need to concentrate on your studies, and not on some ghost story. Kate Shaw was a tragedy for Bard, but we have all moved on." Headmaster B looks at me.

"On the first day of your arrival, I told you that there would be no wasted time at Bard," she says. "Remember the inscription in the Bard chapel? 'I wasted time, and now doth time waste me'? Well, if you have the kind of extra time to perform frivolous séance parties, it appears to me that you have ample time to accomplish something far more rewarding."

"What are you talking about?" Blade asks her.

I already know what she's talking about.

"Chores, my dear. I am talking about chores."

Dish duty is even more disgusting than I could have imagined and I have a very active imagination. There is something really revolting about half-eaten food, and the fact is most of the plates are far from clean. The food is terrible and it looks even worse half-eaten. I'm put at the rinser station, where I'm supposed to rinse off the dishes with a spray nozzle of superhot water. I've got on rubber gloves, but they do little good. I wash dishes for a solid hour and my hands feel red and raw and blistery.

Okay, Mom and Dad. I've learned my lesson, okay? My room is haunted by a temperamental ghost. I'm being stalked by a guy who thinks he's Heathcliff from *Wuthering Heights*. And now I am elbow-deep in the most disgusting, gray, food-blob–filled, rank water ever.

I *get* it. I've done some bad things, and this is karmic payback. And I am really, *truly,* absolutely sorry.

"Whose idea was it to have that séance?" Samir asks as he scrapes off some unknown food particles from a pan in the sink next to mine.

"Your girlfriend's, as I recall," Hana says.

"I'm not his girlfriend," barks Blade, who is towel drying dishes and putting them into the large carts where they're stored.

"Quiet over there!" a Guardian barks at us.

If I ever get home, I think, I'm never going to complain about doing dishes again. Dishes at home = loading dishwasher, and it takes ten minutes. Dishwashing here = scalding-hot water, weird, smelly grayish water with food floating in it, hands so wrinkled they're like prunes, and it takes hours. I am going to vomit.

It is true that I've led a spoiled life. I realize that now. I do. Please. Someone save me.

God doesn't answer my prayer. But he does send me Ryan Kent.

He steps up and puts his tray on the conveyer belt near my rinse station.

I pray that my hair isn't quite flattened to my head with sweat, which is what it feels like. The scalding-hot water has melted all my makeup, I'm sure, and has given my hair the frizz of a Brillo pad.

"Ms. Fashion Police," he says, a look of incredulity on his face. "I can't believe you're on dish duty! What on earth did you do?"

Do I tell him the truth? Yeah, my room is haunted and my crazy Wiccan witch roommate convinced me to do a séance with a Ouija board to try to commune with the dead. You know, because we're insane, hard-core occult nerds. Oh, and by the way, please take my virginity?

"I tried to escape," I lie. Well, technically, it's not exactly a lie. I did try to escape once. It's just not the reason I'm doing dishes.

"You did!" he exclaims. "Wow. I'm impressed. What route did you take?"

"The woods," I say.

"Really? Despite the Kate Shaw legend? You're braver than I am."

Um, yeah, I think, nodding, even though I didn't know about that before I tried the woods on my first night. Still, no point in letting Ryan know that. Let him be impressed.

"I'm not scared by the woods," I say. "You know, I never met a tree I didn't like." I think I might not be making any sense. It's time to dial it down a few notches. I'm having trouble being my usual breezy self. I think it has something to do with the fact that my hands and arms are covered in blobs of watery gravy and bits of spinach.

Not exactly the right accessories for a look of flirty seduction.

"Well, I'm impressed," Ryan says, and he smiles at me, which makes my stomach feel a little like warm oatmeal. He's sort of hanging here a little longer than he should. I'm starting to feel eyes on us. In particular, Parker Rodham's. She has taken notice of us, even though she and her group of friends are sitting down halfway across the cafeteria.

"So," Ryan says.

"So," I say.

An awkward pause ensues. I wonder if he might be trying to tell me I have dish soap on my face.

"Listen, I was wondering, I mean, I guess . . ." Ryan seems a bit flustered. Surely, it can't be that hard to tell me I have soap on my face. Just blurt it out, man!

"I mean, would you, uh, like to go out with me, sometime? I mean, not out out, because you know, we're stuck here, but maybe just hang out or something?"

I'm not positive, but I think in all that babbling somewhere Ryan Kent just asked me out on a date.

"Um, yeah, sure, I mean, yeah, that sounds greattastic," I blurt. What? What the hell did I just say? "Okay, I think I just combined the words 'great' and 'fantastic,' which makes no sense at all."

Ryan Kent laughs, and so do I, and everything is fine.

"So about dinner Saturday night?"

"Perfect. Should I meet you at the cafeteria . . . or at the cafeteria?" I ask, holding up two soapy gloves.

"How about we eat out for a change? Meet me at the chapel at six."

"Eat out? How can we eat out?"

"It'll be a surprise," he says.

"This I have to see," I say.

"Great-tastic," he says, making me laugh.

Sixteen

Who knew that the best and worst day of my life could happen in one week? Go figure. Start out with a haunted room, a séance gone bad, and dish duty, and end up with being asked on a date by Ryan Kent. It just goes to show that even the worst luck has got to turn around sometime.

It's Thursday, technically, so all I have to do is stay out of trouble and make it to Saturday. No more séances. No more communing with ghosts. Out with the Kate Shaw Mystery Society. In with the the Ryan Kent Admiration Society.

My try-to-be-normal plan, however, is strained when Blade puts a clove of garlic under my pillow and it smells like a family-size lasagna has died on my sheets. This also makes my hair smell the same way. I don't know if there's enough Pantene in the world to get out the stink.

"What did you put this here for?" I ask her.

"It's for your protection," she informs me.

"Protection from what? A social life?"

"From the vampire—duh," she says. "I think he's what killed Kate Shaw. It was a vampire. It's all in here."

She holds up her copy of *Dracula*.

"That's it," I say, standing up and taking the book out of her hand. I'm losing my Zen self in a hurry. "I am tired of vampires. I'm tired of ghosts. And I am really starting to get tired of you. I just want everything to be normal for five seconds."

"Jeez. Touchy," Blade says. "If you don't want the garlic protection, then I'll take it. You'll be sorry when you wind up with that bloodsucker on your neck."

"No more vampire talk!" I cry. "It was your séance that got me dish duty, and I don't want to hear anything more about vampires or ghosts or anything that isn't *normal*. If I hear you talk about anything like that, I am taking away this book."

"I'm done reading it, you can have it," Blade says. "I don't really care."

"Fine, I'm taking it then," I say, and put it in my backpack.

"You sure you don't want—?"

"Good night, Blade," I say, jumping into bed and pulling the covers up to my shoulders.

"Suit yourself," Blade says, settling into bed.

After the Blade blowup, I regain my Zen self. The one who isn't letting Blade, or the Kate Shaw mystery, or

Bard academy get to me. All I want to think about is my date. And what I'm going to wear on said date. I don't even want to think about my parents—Dad in particular—or Mom, or how unfair it is that I'm here. I am putting that all aside for the moment. But things aren't Zen for very long.

Friday morning in the bathroom, I bump straight into Parker Rodham and about four members of her clone posse. The Parker Clones look just like Parker Rodham, from their highlighted hair to their Tiffany jewelry. I get the distinct impression this isn't a call from the official welcome committee. Hostility is rolling off them in waves.

This is not something I'm used to. At my old school, the Parker Rodhams loved me. Well, I mean, most everybody loved me. And what's not to love? I'm a nice person. I give free makeovers. But I can tell Parker doesn't want to play nice. This feels like a scene from *Mean Girls*.

"How do you know Ryan?" Parker asks me.

Ryan? Is that what this is about?

"He went to my old school," I say.

"So you must know Rebecca Devon."

Rebecca Devon was Ryan's girlfriend. The one who died in the car crash. Ryan passed an alcohol test, but people still thought it was his fault. He had been the one driving.

"I know of her," I say.

"Well, she used to be my best friend. We saw each

other every summer. Her parents and mine owned houses in Nantucket. We were summer neighbors. I grew up with her *and* Ryan. Our families know each other."

She says this smugly, as if she has the advantage. She's known Ryan longer. Okay, then. I mean, what does she want? A trophy? Congratulations—you played with him in the kiddie pool when you were three? I'm sure that means you're destined to get married.

Okay, I realize that Parker somehow sees me as competition or something, and I'm going to diffuse this situation right now. It's time to be the charming negotiator that I used to be at my old school—the one who managed to convince our old principal to let students leave campus at lunch. I remind myself that I am, after all, the only noncheerleader/nonhonor-student type who had a class president write-in campaign in her honor. I am not the girl who other girls usually hate. I'm the nonthreatening, best-friend type, not the steal-your-boyfriend type. I don't compete for guys. I don't believe in screwing other girls over. I have a strict code of girl ethics. If she has dibs on Ryan, she has dibs. As much as it would pain me to give up my date with him, I would if I thought I was on the wrong side of the girl code.

"Listen, Parker, if this is about Ryan, let's talk about it. I don't know about your history. But I'm a fair-minded person."

Parker's brow furrows and she frowns at me. I guess I said the wrong thing. Usually, when you find yourself in the middle of a boy turf war and you call a truce, the other girl is relieved. Parker just seems pissed.

One of her clones actually barks a laugh. "You can't honestly think Parker is *worried* about you," she says.

"Look at those shoes," another one says, as if this says it all. I glance down at my own brandless ballet flats, and then at their shoes, and realize that they're wearing the shoes I saw in *Teen Vogue* last month. And they're all carrying bags that I dream about: matching Juicy Couture.

They all take a step closer, surrounding me like a pack of hyenas, that is if hyenas wore designer perfume and eight-hundred-dollar shoes.

"Nice leggings," says another girl, of the stretchy black leggings I've started to wear under my skirts. I'm trying to infuse the Bard uniform with style, but it's sort of like trying to give my au natural sister a makeover. It's a losing battle. Luckily, I have lots of hats and jewelry and scarves. I've been rotating through them, trying desperately to look different. If there's one thing I hate more than anything, it's wearing what everybody else is wearing. I'm no clone.

"And nice backpack. What is it? Eddie Bauer?" Another of the clones grabs my backpack off my shoulder and turns it over to see the label. When I try to grab it back, she hands it off to the next clone.

"Come on, guys, are we in a bad made-for TV movie? You can't be serious," I say, reaching for the backpack again just to have it whisked away. Are they going to try to put me in a locker next? I mean, really.

"Just stay away from him, okay?" Parker says. She nods to one of her clones, who drops my backpack in the toilet and then flushes, making sure my backpack gets completely drenched in toilet water.

That is so not cool.

Then the lights above our heads flick off. At first, I think it's Parker's doing and now she and her posse are going to jump on me, but they don't. In fact, they seem as surprised as I am.

"Who did that?" Parker shouts to the bathroom, her voice echoing back from the tiles. When Parker is met with silence, I can tell she, too, gets a little freaked. It's not easy to stand in a pitch-black bathroom and keep your calm.

Parker and her clones aren't used to living in a haunted dorm room like I am. The hand dryers behind them turn on, causing one of Parker's clones to scream. A trashcan is knocked over, too, hitting the floor with a clang. Now everybody's good and spooked.

"Come on, girls, we're done here anyway," Parker says, her voice slightly unnerved. I can tell by the clatter of shoes on the tile that the girls head quickly for the exit, leaving me and my wet backpack in the dark. As soon as they're gone, the lights above me flicker on again.

I can't help but wonder if it's Kate Shaw's ghost.

"If that's you, Kate, thanks," I say to the empty bathroom.

Reluctantly, I pull out my soggy backpack from the toilet. I hate to even look inside, but I do anyway. Most of my homework is ruined, as well as my spiral notebooks that I use to take notes. There goes pretty much all of my work for midterms. You know, a month's worth of work literally down the toilet.

I look at my soggy special history report for Coach H that I was supposed to turn in today. The ink has run down the pages, and they're all stuck together in a great, soggy mess. Somehow I doubt he's going to believe me when I tell him what happened to my homework assignment.

"My bully flushed it" doesn't sound too credible.

I try to be Zen about it, but all I can think is that I want to make Parker Rodham the next Bard Academy ghost. With my bare hands.

Seventeen

Hana consoles me by offering to take me to the Bard Academy bookstore Saturday afternoon, the only shop on campus, to replace my lost notebooks and backpack.

"Unless there's a fully written report and extra credit to make up for the F Coach H is going to give me for my ruined report, then I don't think the store is going to help me," I tell Hana.

"Come on, I'll buy you a smiley-face sticker," she says.

"How about some rat poison for Parker Rodham instead?"

"Maybe you need two smiley-face stickers."

The bookstore is a relatively small room: it makes a Citgo gas station look like the Mall of America. It has pens, pencils, notepads (all with the Bard Academy logo on them, as if you could forget where you are), backpacks, and replacement uniforms. There are also rows of books, divided by class. No money is ever exchanged at the bookstore, because students aren't allowed to have cash. They think it will tempt us to attempt to run away. So you sign off on everything and I suppose they'll bill your parents later. I secretly hope the Bard Academy supplies I intend to buy (the folders, notebooks, and pens) cost my dad a fortune. It would serve him right for sending me here in the first place.

Not to mention, if my new backpack costs one thousand dollars then he'd be here tomorrow to get me. Dad has a thing about money. Only he and his newest wife can spend it. Everyone else has to cut coupons and shop at the thrift store.

Dad, by the way, has yet to write. He's probably in the middle of another divorce proceeding. That, or another affair. Like Mom says, he's got the emotional maturity of a twelve-year-old. This reminds me that I need to write him a letter. I haven't made any progress on it at all.

Hana goes off to the pen and pencil aisle to look for a protractor and I'm left studying the other backpacks, trying to figure out which one would be the most expensive, when I hear the faint sound of laughter. It sounds an awful lot like what I heard in the bathroom before someone set fire to my trashcan.

The sound of laughter is definitely getting louder. I step behind the backpack display trying to figure out if it's coming from the grate or not, when I bump straight into . . . Heathcliff.

It's like hitting a wall, he's so broad and tall.

"I'm sorry," I say, realizing belatedly that I'm standing on his foot. Literally, *standing* on it. He doesn't even flinch. It's like he doesn't even feel my weight on his foot. This is how tough he is.

Suddenly, the strong smell of burning fabric hits me.

"Do you smell something . . . ?" Before I can finish my question, he's got his arm around me and is pushing me aside.

"What are you . . . ?" I protest, just as he shoves me into the folders aisle. That's when I look up and see that the backpacks above me are on fire. The top few topple off the rack like fire bombs, hitting the floor with a crackle and sending off sparks at the exact spot where I was standing before Heathcliff pushed me out of the way.

Someone else in the store screams and then other people start to run. Heathcliff stomps on the backpacks, suffocating the fire. In seconds, the flames are out.

"Cathy . . ." he calls to me, just as Guardians rush into the store.

"But, I'm not . . ." I start, as Heathcliff runs out and the Guardians run after him. "Cathy," I finish.

I glance down at the floor and realize that Heathcliff has dropped his silver lighter near the backpacks. I reach down and snatch it up from the ground.

I have a sudden thought: Is Heathcliff the one who set the fire? This one and the one in my dorm? But then,

I remember I heard a girl's laughter before I smelled the smoke in both cases. That's certainly not him.

"Wow, that was close," Hana says to me outside the bookstore. "You almost got hit."

"I know, but Heathcliff saved me," I say, slipping the lighter into my pocket. I fiddle with it in my pocket. It's cold and hard.

"Who's Heathcliff?" Hana asks.

"The guy who was late to assembly the first day? You remember him?"

"Vaguely," Hana says. "What's his story?"

"I wish I knew," I say. "I think he's obsessed with *Wuthering Heights*. I know it sounds crazy, but I think he's trying to be Heathcliff from the book. He says he's from *Wuthering Heights,* and that he's an orphan."

"A thug at this school is obsessed with classic lit?"

"I know. It sounds insane."

"Sounds more than insane. Sounds impossible."

"Yeah, I know. I can't figure it out," I say. "But he saved me from dish duty on the first day of classes, and just now he rescued me from the backpack fireball."

"Sounds like he tends to be in the right place at the right time," Hana says.

"Or the wrong place at the wrong time, depending on how you look at it," I say. "What if he's the one who set the fire?"

"You think this guy is a pyromaniac?"

"I don't know," I say. "I really don't."

. . .

After the bookstore fire, there are two more fires on campus—one in the boys' dorm, and one in Hana's classroom. A rumor starts that the campus has an arsonist on the loose. Soon after, the Guardians sweep through the dorms, confiscating anything that might be used to cause a fire. It shows how not-thorough the first pat-downs were, because they gather up tons of lighters, matches, candles, and other contraband. Even Blade has to give up her skull candle. I, for one, am not sad to see it go.

And as if this isn't bad enough, a girl faints in our dorm, and she is carried out of the dorm on a stretcher, which is a bit unnerving. Her roommate says she hasn't been eating, but Blade thinks she's been attacked by the vampire she's obsessed with.

"It's Dracula for sure," Blade says. "I know because he does the green mist thing. I've seen it."

"You've *seen* it?" I ask, skeptical.

"Okay, well, *I* didn't see it, but the girl who fainted said she saw green mist."

"Maybe that's because she hasn't eaten in a week," I say.

"Or because she got drained by Dracula," Blade says.

"And just why do you think the baddest vampire in the world is hanging out at a boarding school?"

"What can I say? He likes young chicks. I guess their blood tastes better."

"You are deeply disturbed," I say.

"Funny. That's what my ex-boyfriend said," Blade says as she grabs her backpack and heads out of our room. "I'm going to the library. If Dracula stops by, I've left some holy water on the desk."

"Gee, thanks," I say.

Eighteen

I decide not to let Blade's vampire obsession distract me from more important issues—namely, what I'm going to wear to meet Ryan tonight. Since Parker Rodham rejected my offer of a boy truce, then I can go on the date guilt-free. And I refuse to let Parker, or ghosts, or vampires, ruin this date.

I start trying on outfits and go through everything I brought with me.

"Satan, what do you think?" I ask Blade's poster, doing a little fashion catwalk wearing my minidress. I glance at him and then down at my dress. "You're right. Trying too hard."

I change into jeans—which are clearly not trying hard enough—and quickly run through all my outfits. Eventually, I just settle on the Bard uniform. It has the benefit of a) not trying too hard, and b) preventing me from getting detention should I be caught by a Guardian. Not wearing your uniform on campus is a detention-worthy offense.

I take special care with my makeup and decide on a chunky necklace instead of my tie, my knee-high black boots instead of my socks and sneakers.

Blade is out at the library, so I'm alone in the room. It's only me and Satan.

"So, Satan, how do I look?" I ask the poster. He just grins at me with his devilish grin. I take that as a good sign. Lucifer approves.

The bell outside tolls. It's six! I'm late.

Even as I sprint out of the dorm (and by sprint, I mean walk really fast. I don't run unless someone is chasing me), I pray that I look okay, given the fact that the dorm light is terrible and I didn't have any hairspray (all flammable items were confiscated during the Bard arsonist-related sweeps of the dorms).

I glance up at the big clock tower above the chapel, some distance away, and it says five past. I'm late! I'm walking as fast as possible, given that my heart is about to explode. I suspect I look like Mom when she tries to powerwalk around the neighborhood. It was one of her workout fads. Mom bought special fast-walk jogging suits and shorts, as well as funky-looking neon green-and-pink tennis shoes. She even had a fanny pack for a water bottle. But like all her previous workout endeavors (Pilates, yoga, tennis, spinning, and rebounding), it lasted for all of about a week and a half before she grew bored with it and quit. And she says I'm the one who has no patience.

My pace slows as the chapel looms in front of me. I hesitate. Is it worse to stand Ryan up, or show up looking and/or smelling like I've not showered in days? Before I can decide, Ryan steps out from the shadows, a smile on his face.

"I thought you weren't going to show," he says, looking relieved. He was actually *worried.* Wow. He might really be human after all. "You look great-tastic," he says, making me smile.

"Come on. I've got a surprise for you," he says and grabs my hand. I'm too shocked by the contact of my skin on his to do anything but follow him. I keep staring at his hand covering mind, thinking, Ryan Kent is holding my hand. Someone call CNN, because I want the whole world to know.

Ryan's hand is warm and strong, and I want him to hold mine forever. I try to act like this isn't a big deal, even though my heart is beating a hundred times a minute. I want to scream, "Ryan Kent is holding my hand! He's holding it! ON PURPOSE!" at the top of my lungs, but I know that this won't help my cause and would probably just summon a bunch of Guardians, who would lock us up in our respective dorm rooms.

Granted, we're not technically in violation of curfew—yet. I've got another hour and Ryan (as an upperclassman) has two. Ryan takes me around the chapel to the back entrance and pulls me through the back door.

Once inside, I expect him to drop my hand, but he doesn't. He's holding it tightly as he takes me back to the staircase behind the altar. It's too cold out for our palms to start sweating. I keep wondering if I'm holding on to him too tightly or not tightly enough. There is a gentle compromise with hand holding. Granted, it's a lot simpler than kissing, but there's still an art to it.

Of all the weirdness of this school—Heathcliff, Kate Shaw, the séance-gone-bad, or Parker and her bullies—I have to say that Ryan Kent holding my hand for—going on ten minutes—is by far the strangest. A year ago, if you'd told me that I'd be holding hands with Ryan Kent in the back of a dark church in a place called Shipwreck Island, I would've told you to check yourself into a mental institution.

We walk up the winding enclosed staircase, with the large bell swaying slightly above our heads and the white light of the clock tower casting a glow on the stairs. It's cozy up here and not scary like you'd think, although it would probably have a serious creep factor if Ryan weren't here. But with him, I feel like nothing bad could ever happen to me.

Ryan drops my hand and shrugs off his backpack. I try not to be disappointed by the feel of the cool air on my palm. It's not like we could eat and hold hands at the same time. Well, not comfortably anyway. Ryan opens up his backpack and takes out a towel and a brown bag, and then he produces a three-course meal: Fritos, Pop-Tarts, and two Snickers bars.

"Where did you get all this?" I ask him, as if he's just produced a Thanksgiving turkey dinner.

"Contraband," Ryan says. "There are some kids on campus selling food and electronics."

He pulls out his iPod next, along with a special stand to sit it on with minispeakers.

"I wasn't sure about what mood music goes with Pop-Tarts," he says. "But I figure everything goes with Death Cab for Cutie."

"I LOVE Death Cab for Cutie," I exclaim, giving him a playful shove. I like the excuse to make physical contact with him.

"You're not just saying that, are you?" he asks me.

"Are you kidding? If you're about to play 'Soul Meets Body,' then we are soul mates."

I suck in my breath for a second after the sentence is out of my mouth. Did I go too far? It's practically a step away from declaring my undying love for Ryan Kent *to his face.* But Ryan doesn't seem to be put off. He quirks an eyebrow at me, just as the first chords of "Soul Meets Body" start.

I smile and he smiles back. I definitely feel a date vibe. Not, of course, that I'd *know* what a date vibe was, exactly. My mom has this rule that I can't go out on dates until I'm sixteen. Group dates—the sort where you, your beloved, and about fifteen of your closest friends pile into a movie theater or a mall (or both, in most cases)—are fine. But one-on-one dates are off-limits until I'm driving age.

I don't feel bad about violating Mom's Cardinal Dating Rule (which is "You can't kiss a boy in a car until you're old enough to drive one around") because, after all, she sent me off to this place. I've had to grow up fast. I'm sure in mental years, with my parents' divorce, wrecking my dad's car, a near rape, and the Bard Academy exile, I'm probably hovering somewhere at thirty-two.

I never thought I'd be so glad to see Pop-Tarts or Fritos, but I devour them.

"Oh my God, I have died and gone to heaven," I say, grabbing chips and launching them into my mouth at speeds better suited for NASCAR. It occurs to me mid-bite that shoving chips into my mouth by the handful probably isn't very ladylike or attractive. But I can't help it, I'm starved.

"Wow, you're eating this stuff," he says, looking like he's never seen a girl eat before. Then again, given Parker and her anorexic groupies, maybe he's not used to seeing girls eat.

"Igh dat a problem?" I mumble, mouth full.

"No, no, not at all. I like girls who eat. I feel less like the pig I am," he says, taking a huge bite of cherry Pop-Tart.

"Okay, is it just me, or were Pop-Tarts always the best food on earth and I just never knew it?"

"Best food ever," Ryan agrees, nodding.

We eat and talk as if we're the best of friends and I'm immediately at ease. Of course, if I look too long at Ryan's face I find myself compelled to stare. It's hard not to do. He's that good looking.

I don't know if I'm feeling brave because of the carbs now gushing through my system, wrecking more havoc I'm sure than Everclear, but I feel calm, almost even *comfortable* with Ryan Kent.

"By the way, how much did this dinner cost you?" I ask him.

"You don't want to know."

"'Fess up."

"Forty bucks," he says.

"You can't be serious! This whole thing probably didn't cost ten."

Ryan shrugs. "I never skimp on dates," he says.

"Wow, you used the D word," I say. "I thought guys didn't use the D word anymore." It's true. Most guys will go to any length not to refer to an outing as a "date." It's "hanging out" or "going to a movie" or "chilling," but it's *never* a date. "I thought the D word makes things too serious."

"I don't mind serious," Ryan says. My stomach goes all warm and gooey. And that, I'm pretty sure, has nothing to do with the Pop-Tarts.

When we reach for, and grab, the same Frito, it has the feeling of *Lady and the Tramp.* I don't let go and neither does he. A sly smile crosses his face.

"Should we wrestle for it?" he asks me, and I laugh. He pulls on the Frito a little, causing me to move forward. I realize suddenly that I'm very close to Ryan Kent, and that he has stopped smiling and he's looking at me seriously.

"Miranda . . ." he starts, and it's at this moment that I'm completely sucked into Ryan's brown puppy dog eyes. I want to swim in them, they're so warm and luscious. They seem to be moving closer and then I realize *they are* moving closer.

It hits me like a bolt of lightning: Ryan Kent is going to *kiss* me.

Nineteen

A word about my kissing experience.

This is embarrassing, since some of my friends (Cass and Liz) have claimed with pride to be kissing hos (and in Liz's case, just plain ho), I have only had one legitimate kiss on the lips my whole life (not counting the drunken smear that Tyler tried to land—unsuccessfully—on me in his Toyota Forerunner).

My legitimate—as in consensual—kiss happened three years ago.

I think this could pretty much make me into a kissing virgin again, considering my memory of "the kiss" (with Gregory Mason, my seventh grade "boyfriend" of five weeks) is vague at best. Basically, it happened in my room, after Gregory had come over to do math homework, and Coldplay was blaring. My door was open (per Mom's rules), but she was too busy talking on the phone to one of her friends about the pros and cons of liposuction to pay much attention to what was happening in my room, and Lindsay (thank God) was at softball practice.

Gregory had put down his pencil and said, "You wanna kiss?" just like he'd asked me if I wanted a piece of gum. I said, "Okay," and then Gregory had smashed his face into mine at high velocity. Then, for good measure, he'd thrust out his tongue three times, just like a lizard. The first time, he hit my lower lip, the second time my upper teeth, and the third landed a direct blow to my tongue itself with such force it felt like he was trying to wrestle my tongue to the roof of my mouth.

I later heard from other girls that this was Gregory's patented technique. Three lizard-tongue thrusts. Based on the way these girls (admitted lip hos) laughed at Gregory, I'm guessing his approach wasn't very good. Of course, I could tell this myself. I'm still wondering how a boy's tongue could be so pointy.

So I don't have much experience in the kissing department, and that's because I'm exceptionally picky about the people I choose to go with. So sue me. I mean, I won't go with just any boy who asks me. Not that I've had a *ton* of boys ask me freshman year, but I did get a few offers, just not of the caliber I would accept.

And now here is Ryan Kent, sitting nearly nose-to-nose with me, his lips slightly parted and no words coming out. I'm leaning in to him, or he's leaning in to me, I can't tell which, and it feels like everything in the world has been paused TiVo-style. I want this moment to last absolutely forever.

That's when I hear it. The soft sound of laughter. Girl-maniacal laughter. I freeze. Does Ryan hear it, too? Or is this just my overactive imagination again?

The girl's laughter gets louder.

The spell, or whatever it was between us, breaks, as Ryan looks up.

"Do you hear that?" he asks me.

"You hear it, too?" I exclaim, relieved. Maybe I'm not actually going crazy. "I thought I was imagining it."

"No, I definitely hear it," Ryan says. "Who do you think it is?"

"I don't know, but every time I hear it . . ." Before I can even finish my sentence, the smell of smoke reaches my nose. "I think it's the Bard arsonist."

"The kid setting fires?" Ryan asks, starting to look alarmed.

"I think we ought to get out of here, quickly," I say, pulling Ryan to his feet.

"Hey—is something burning?"

"Yeah, it could be us, if we don't get out of here."

Ryan sweeps his iPod into his backpack and crumples up the garbage as he grabs my hand. I'm too busy being happy in the knowledge that I'm once again touching Ryan Kent to be too disturbed by the fact that this whole place may soon go up in flames. I realize this is wrong. But what can I do? I *am* a girl, after all.

The smoke starts to get thicker, and as we make our

way down the stairs I hear laughter above us. It sounds closer than it's ever been. When I look up I see a crazed-looking woman in a white nightgown. Her hair is a mess and she has a wild look in her eye. I've never seen her before. She's peering at us over the railing; when she sees me looking at her, she just starts to laugh.

The *laugh*. It's the same laugh I've heard before every fire. The maniacal, I'm-crazy laugh. That's it. It's her. This woman in the nightgown. As I watch, she backs away and runs upward—toward the fire. You know, because people who walk around with crazy hair in white nightgowns are probably—what's the word I'm looking for—*insane*?

Still, I can't just let her die, even if she is a crazy person.

"Wait," I cry, tugging on Ryan's arm. "There's a woman up there. A woman by the fire."

Ryan slows. "We were just up there, there wasn't a woman," he says.

"I saw a woman."

"Hello?" Ryan calls upward. No one answers. The smoke is so thick now that I start to cough. "Maybe I should go see."

Ryan rips off his sweater and puts it across his face as he rushes, without hesitation, straight up the stairs. Of course he would moonlight as a superhero.

"Ryan! Ryan . . .wait!"

I watch him as he climbs up the stairs. What have I done? If that's the crazy arsonist, then Ryan is going to be in serious trouble. It's now so smoky that I can't see the upper landing, or Ryan, at all.

"Ryan! Are you okay? Ryan!"

I start to move up the stairs when two strong hands grab me from behind. I turn to see Heathcliff there.

Of course he's here. He's always around when fires start, a nagging voice in my head tells me.

"Let go of me," I cry, tugging hard against him, but he's too strong for me.

"Cathy, we have to go!"

"I'm not *Cathy,*" I cry, fighting him harder.

"I have to get you out of here, *now.*"

"I'm not going without Ryan."

"Forget him," Heathcliff says, frowning.

"I'm not leaving without him. Either you help me get him or I'm getting him by myself."

Heathcliff loosens his grip. "You know that anything you tell me to do, I'll do."

"Then help Ryan."

Heathcliff frowns at me, but then he turns and runs up the stairs, his arm covering his mouth. Is it possible? Does Heathcliff *do my bidding?* No one does my bidding. Not even Lindsay. Or should I say, especially not Lindsay.

I'm starting to get light-headed from the smoke. Seconds later, Heathcliff appears, and he's got Ryan slung over his shoulder.

"Come on," he says, grabbing me by the arm and leading me forward.

Outside the chapel, Heathcliff carries Ryan over to a nearby tree and lays him down, scowling as he does so. Even good deeds don't make Heathcliff happy.

"Miranda? Is that you? God, what happened?" Hana cries, running up to me. Samir isn't far behind. I guess they were in the library, because that's the direction from which they're coming.

"Are you okay? And who's this?" Samir asks, pointing at Heathcliff.

"I . . ." I am light-headed, is what I am. The smoke . . . and everything. My throat closes up and I start to cough, and then I can't stop. It takes hold of my chest and shakes me so hard that I feel like someone has a vise grip on my bronchial tubes. Heathcliff's head shoots up and I see him walk over to me, a concerned look on his face.

I double over, I'm coughing so hard, and I wonder when I'll be able to stop. That's the last thing I remember thinking before I pass out.

Twenty

I wake up on a stretcher in the infirmary. It's a large room with several cots and at least three private exam rooms with doors. It's the most brightly lit room at Bard, with fluorescent lights above me. It looks like a mini-emergency room. I can't help but wonder why they have such a big infirmary.

The first thing I hear is Samir's voice. "I've never seen anyone faint before," he says.

"Ugh?" I grumble, meaning to form words, but my throat feels like someone took my tonsils out without any anesthetic. I guess it was the smoke I inhaled in the chapel.

"You fainted," Hana says.

"Dropped like a stone," Samir agrees. "By the way, you are heavier than you look."

"You caught me?" I croak, sounding like either Patty or Selma from *The Simpsons*.

"No, your friend did. He carried you all the way here." I look over and see that Heathcliff is staring at me, doing his strong-and-silent routine while sitting outside the infirmary on a bench in the hall, as Coach H and Ms. W attempt to interrogate him. He won't look at them, just at me. Samir continues, "I'm just *guessing* you're heavier than you look, based on, well, looks."

"Shut up, Samir," I say. "You are so like a little brother sometimes."

"I know. It's one of my most charming qualities."

"What are they doing?" I ask Hana, looking over at Heathcliff.

"They're trying to figure out what happened," Hana says. "But he's not being very helpful—big surprise."

I cough a little, but recover. I feel totally crappy. My throat is burning and my head feels like I'm having the worst caffeine-withdrawal headache ever.

"What about Ryan?"

"He's fine. He's over there," Hana says, pointing to one of the closed-door exam rooms. "He's resting."

I sit up, thinking I'll go over and try to talk to him, but I'm stopped mid sit-up by a sharp, blinding headache.

"Ow," I cry, holding my head and slowly laying back down on the cot.

"Coach H warned us that might happen," Samir says. "You shouldn't move too quickly."

"Nice of you to tell me now," I say, "when it does me absolutely no good. And what does he know about it?"

"He doubles as the school nurse," Samir says, which

causes me to laugh. Only the laugh turns into a cough, and then a wheeze.

"Oh, don't make me laugh, it hurts," I say, putting a hand to my chest, which feels like it's on fire.

"I'm serious. He *is* the school nurse. He told us he drove an ambulance in the war."

"War? What war? The Gulf War?"

"I don't know. I didn't ask him," Samir says.

"Never mind that," Hana says. "I think you'll want to know that we found out something else about your friend over there." She nods her head in Heathcliff's direction. "He's not a student here."

"What do you mean?"

"We overheard his conversation with Coach. Bard has no record of him."

"Why is he here then?" I ask.

"Nobody knows," Samir says. "He won't even give his name, but Hana said you know him."

"I don't know him," I say. "Not really."

"Who just shows up out of nowhere at Bard?" Hana asks.

"And pretending to be a literary character from the 1800s, don't forget," I say.

"I'm missing something," Samir says.

"I'll fill you in later," Hana says.

"In any case, he *seriously* digs you," Samir adds, in case it wasn't already obvious.

"What clued you into that?" Hana asks him sarcastically. "Him saving Miranda from a stack of burning backpacks, or just now when he pulled her and her date from the burning chapel?"

"I'm just saying, maybe Miranda didn't notice. She did pass out. She could have memory loss."

I noticed. I definitely noticed.

"Do you still think he's the one setting fires?" Hana asks me.

"He's what?" Samir exclaims. "Why doesn't anyone tell me anything?"

"I don't know. I'm beginning to think that the arsonist is a woman. Before the fire, I saw a crazy woman in a white nightgown. She was laughing. But it's the same laugh I've been hearing near other fires."

"Sounds like Mrs. Rochester," Hana says.

"Who?" Samir asks.

"Mrs. Rochester. From *Jane Eyre*?" Hana explains. "It's my favorite book."

"*Jane Eyre* is your favorite book? You are such a nerd," Samir says.

"That's rich coming from you, Mr. I Collect *Lord of the Rings* Toys."

"Can we get back to this Mrs. Rochester character?" I ask the two of them.

"Jane Eyre is a governess who goes to work in the house of Mr. Rochester," Hana says. "The two of them fall in love, but what Jane Eyre doesn't know is that Mr. Rochester has a crazy wife he locked in the attic. She's insane, and she laughs all the time, and well, she . . . sets fires."

"Nice love story," I say.

"It is a weird coincidence," Hana says. "Heathcliff trying to be Heathcliff, and then this woman trying to be Mrs. Rochester."

"What is this? Some new psychological condition?" Samir says. "Like schizophrenia, only with literature— Shakespearenia?"

Suddenly, behind us, the conversation of Heathcliff and Coach H gets louder. It's an argument.

"Tell us where she is," Coach says, nearly at a shout. "Where is Emily? Where is she?"

Who's Emily?

"I'll not tell you anything, you milk-blooded coward," Heathcliff says.

That's when Coach H rears back and strikes Heathcliff. Actually hits him straight across the face. Headmaster B gasps.

I'm stunned, and Samir and Hana are speechless. That has got to violate some cardinal campus rule about teacher-student relations.

Heathcliff, for his part, doesn't even flinch or even make a sound. He just spits at the feet of Coach H, as if to say, "That's the best you can do?"

"I'll tell you nothing," Heathcliff says in low tones. Then he puts both hands on H's shoulders and shoves him hard into the Guardians, who are supposed to be keeping watch. As the three stumble and fall, he runs the other way toward the exit. He pauses there before he leaves, looking straight at me. He doesn't smile, he just meets my eye for a fraction of a second, and then he's gone.

I definitely don't want to get on that boy's bad side, I think. He's a force to be reckoned with.

"Your boyfriend is some kind of badass," Samir says.

"He's not my boyfriend," I say, but even I'm not exactly sure if that's true.

Headmaster B and Coach H draw closer together and speak in urgent whispers. They're joined shortly in the hall by Ms. W, who seems pretty upset by Heathcliff's disappearance. I can't hear what they're saying, but they seem worried. A bit frantic, even. They start to argue. They can't seem to agree on what to do next. Headmaster B leaves.

"Something is definitely up," Samir says. "They look worried."

Coach and Ms. W finally take notice of us, and the fact that I'm sitting up and conscious.

"You," Coach says, pointing. "You need to tell us everything."

After I recount my version of the story, Coach says, "I told you it was her," as if he knew about our Mrs. Rochester lookalike.

"We have a serious problem on our hands," Ms. W says. "Has someone checked the vault? If any more books are out . . ." she trails off.

Why is she talking about books? I look at Hana and Samir and they're both equally confused.

"Coach," calls one of the Guardians, "we found it." They hold up my backpack and Kate Shaw's ripped-out page of *Wuthering Heights* that I found in my closet. I'd been using it as a bookmark for one of my other books.

Ms. W and Coach rush over. Coach carefully takes the page from the Guardian's hands, as if it were a delicate treasure. He inspects it.

Coach turns to me and shouts, "Where did you get this?" His face is red and he's angry. Very angry. "Do you have any idea how dangerous this is? You could've been killed. You could've killed someone else. You could've destroyed everything . . ." he thunders at me.

Destroyed everything? How? It's just a piece of paper. The most serious threat it poses, as far as I can tell, is the possibility of a paper cut.

Ms. W puts her hand on Coach's arm, as if to warn him he's about to reveal too much.

"Coach H doesn't like vandalism of books," Ms. W says, smoothly interrupting Coach's rant. "And this comes from a very rare first edition. It's irreplaceable."

Don't ask me why, but I think she's lying, or at least leaving something out. Coach is acting like this page is a weapon of mass destruction. There's something they're not telling us.

"Now, this is very important. Tell us how you came into possession of this page."

"My closet," I say, which has them both puzzled. That's when I tell them about Kate Shaw's ghost.

I expect them to laugh at me. I mean, you don't normally expect a pair of adults to take a ghost story seriously. But, like Headmaster B, they listen to every word, not once telling me I'm being silly or imagining things.

I get to the part about the key and pull it from my pocket, then tell them about the séance and Kate telling us the key goes to the greenhouse.

"The greenhouse," Ms. W says to Coach.

"That's where she is," Coach says, grabbing the key from my hand.

"Where who is? Kate?" I ask, confused.

They ignore me. They both stand up, as if they have to leave. And I haven't even finished the story.

"You have to stay here," Ms. W says. "We have some business to take care of. Samir and Hana, look after Miranda, all right?"

"Virginia, you're wasting time we don't have," Coach H thunders at her by the door. "Come on."

"The three of you stay together," Ms. W says. "If you see Heathcliff, *do not approach him.* He is very dangerous. If you see him, hide."

"Why?" I ask. "Is he the Bard arsonist?"

"No time to explain," she says. "The three of you stay together, and stay here. Whatever you do, don't go outside. We'll be back as soon as we can."

"But why?"

Ms. W doesn't answer us. She runs after Coach and the two of them head out of the infirmary in a rush. In fact, they leave in such a hurry that Coach H unknowingly drops Kate's key, the one to the greenhouse.

"What the hell was all that about?" Samir asks.

"I have no idea," Hana says.

"We should follow them," I say.

"Why?"

"For one thing, they forgot the key," I say, pointing to the key on the floor. "What do you say? You guys feel like taking a little trip?"

"But they told us to stay put," Hana says.

"Since when do we follow the rules? We're delinquents," I say, quoting Samir.

As we start to get up, one of the private exam doors open. I look up, expecting (and hoping) to see Ryan Kent. Instead, Blade walks out.

"I heard everything," she says. "And you're not going without me."

"Blade! What are you doing here?"

"Dracula," she said, pointing to a bandage on her neck. "The jerk managed to get me tonight. I'd probably be the undead by now, except that Ms. W saved me and brought me here."

"Dracula? Are you serious?" Hana sounds very skeptical.

"What? You believe in ghosts, but not in vampires? Please," Blade says. "And anyway, here's proof." She pulls off the bandage and shows us two red fang holes. They are still fresh and bleeding.

"Ouch," Samir says.

"FYI," Blade adds, "garlic and protection spells don't work worth a crap against vampires. I'm going to have to petition the Wiccan counsel on that one."

Hana and I stare at each other. Dracula? Why not? Add it to the mix of the bizarre around here.

"So are we going to go to this greenhouse or what?" Blade asks us, as she puts her neck bandage back in place.

Twenty-one

"Whose idea was this again?" Samir asks us, as the four of us stand in front of the greenhouse on the edge of campus. He's clearly a little nervous. It's probably the fact that we're so far away from the other school buildings that we're practically in the woods.

In the distance, a wolf howls.

It's the middle of the night. Hana rubs her arms to ward off the chill and looks anxiously around us. The campus greenhouse is an old, wrought-iron building the size of most gymnasiums. It's covered in fog and has a dim light coming from the inside. On the outside door, the sign reads DANGER—DO NOT ENTER.

Blade tries the door. "It's locked," she says.

"Really? That's too bad," Samir says, turning around. "I guess we'll have to go."

"Not so fast," I say, putting my hand on Samir's chest and pushing him back a little. "I have a key, remember?"

I take Kate's key out of my pocket and slide it into the lock. It turns and the door creaks open.

"You were saying?" I say. I make a move to go in and Samir grabs my arm.

"You're not seriously going in there?" Samir asks us, looking a bit hesitant. "I mean, this building looks like it's going to fall down. I bet it's condemned."

As we're standing there, in fact, one of the hinges to the door falls off, causing the door to hit the ground with a thud. We all jump back a little.

"See?" Samir says.

"I'm going in anyway," I say. I feel like I owe it to Kate.

Inside, a wall of humid heat and the almost-too-sweet smell of orchids washes over us. The glass walls are covered in thick condensation and it's hard to see. There are shelves inside, lined with plants.

"It's in use; it's not deserted," I say to them. "You guys coming or not?"

Hana steps in after me.

"Come on, you chicken," Blade says, grabbing Samir's hand and pulling him inside the greenhouse. I can tell Samir is torn—his hormones are in overdrive since Blade is holding his hand, but he's also really scared of the dark. His hormones eventually win and he follows us in.

The dim lights we saw from the outside are coming from rows of long, skinny lamps up over the plants themselves, as a kind of twenty-four-hour sunshine.

There isn't any sign of Coach H or Ms. W. They must be at some other part of the greenhouse, or maybe still looking for a way in.

I glance over at the stone statues of children beside me. Something about their blank-faced expressions make me think of ghosts. I shiver. Something about this place isn't right. It definitely isn't right.

"See? I told you. Nobody is here. Why don't we leave now?" Samir asks us.

"Shhhh," Blade says.

"This would make a perfect make-out spot for you and one of your freshmen," Hana says.

"Freshmen?" Blade asks.

"Oh yeah, I have at least three or four of them who are after me," Samir says.

"Yeah, they're after you to do their homework," Hana says.

The greenhouse is huge. The rows go on for what seems like miles. There's no sign of Coach H or Ms. W. As far as I can tell, the only living things in the greenhouse are plants and us.

"What are we looking for?" Hana asks.

"I think we'll know it when we find it," I say.

We start walking along a line of rosebushes, their thorns nearly as big as the flowers. Farther down in the row, I start to see plants I've never seen before. The flowers are bright magenta, deep blue, neon green. There's one flower that looks like a snake rearing its head.

"Wow. Cool," exclaims Blade, picking it up.

It's green and red and has a little red slit that looks like a mouth. And it might be my imagination, but it seems like it might be, well, *moving*.

"I don't think you should pick that up," Hana cautions. I have to agree. It's not the sort of thing I want to see close-up.

Blade reaches out with her other hand to touch the green petals. Then, in a blink of an eye, the bud snaps shut on her finger.

"Ow," she cries, dropping the flowerpot to the ground. It breaks with a clatter, sending dirt flying in all directions. On the ground, the plant is definitely squirming, as if it's alive, its roots and petals whipping about. "It *bit* me," Blade exclaims, showing us her finger. There's a little red ring there and a tiny drop of blood.

"Weird," Samir says. Blade isn't going to let the attack slide. She slams her foot down on the squirming plant, flattening it underneath her Doc Martens lace-up boot. It makes a sickening, squishing sound, sending green-and-black goo in all directions.

"Gross," Hana says.

Blade scrapes her boot against the ground, leaving a trail of black-and-green plant guts. I just stare at her. I still can't quite believe she killed it.

"What?" she asks me. "I'm tired of being on the freakin' menu."

"Come on, let's keep going."

In the distance we hear voices, and then something

that sounds like a crash. It sounds like Ms. W and Coach H for sure, and then someone else I don't recognize. The four of us sneak down the aisle and then hide behind a row of ferns to try to get a better look.

There's a sitting room and Ms. W and Coach H are there. They're talking to another woman. She's dressed in all black.

"Emily, you know this is forbidden," Ms. W says. "These characters do not belong in this dimension. They have to go back."

"They are not characters, they are *people,* and I am freeing them," Emily says.

"You're attaching them to *students,* Emily, and you know the dangers of this," Coach H says. "You have to stop it at once. You have to come with us."

"I am not going anywhere but home," Emily says. "I'm not going anywhere but the Moors."

And as we watch, Emily reaches into her pocket and pulls out two books. They are old, with tattered covers, and writing that's so worn on the outsides I can't quite tell what they are.

"How did you get those? That's impossible . . ." I hear Ms. W shout, but it's the last thing she says coherently. Emily opens one of the books and, as we watch, Ms. W is sucked into it, like it's a black hole. Literally— *sucked in. Slurp.* Gone.

"Cool," whispers Blade, not at all scared—naturally. Anything occult she's all over.

"What the . . ." Samir shouts, giving away our position and temporarily drawing the attention of Coach H and the woman called Emily.

Emily uses the distraction to open the other book and suck in Coach H, as well, like he was a piece of dust being picked up by a Hoover. *Pfffffffffft.* Gone.

"Children," Emily says to us. "Come in. I've been expecting you." Emily seems to be struggling to hold on to the books, as if they are fighting against her hands, trying to open themselves. Every so often, I see a handprint come out from a side of one of the books, as if Ms. W or Coach H are fighting to be free. Eventually, she puts them on the ground and puts a heavy terracotta pot on top of them. It seems to take care of the squirming books, which are pinned fast to the ground.

"What is going on?" I ask Emily. "Who are you? And what did you do to our teachers?"

"Why, dear girl, you don't recognize me? Not from the Bard yearbook you've been carrying around?"

I shake my head.

"Well, I am disappointed," Emily says. "I thought you were a bit smarter, Ms. Tate. I'm Emily Brontë."

"The Emily Brontë who wrote *Wuthering Heights*?" I echo, not sure I'm understanding what's going on. "The Emily Brontë who died in 1848?"

"The same," she says, and takes a little bow.

"But that's . . ."

"Impossible?" Emily says. "Impossible like imprisoning your teachers in books is impossible?"

"You're a ghost!" exclaims Blade. "Wow, this is, like, *totally awesome*." Naturally, she isn't the least bit scared. I'm sure meeting dead people is Blade's dream come true. She'll have to add it to her MySpace list of "turn-ons."

"Is she a ghost? Because if she is, I'm going to have a freak-out moment," Samir says.

"You're not a ghost," Hana says. "You're just some crazy woman. I don't believe a word of it."

Emily Brontë shakes her head sadly. "You children today are so very skeptical. It's no wonder there's such a dearth of good fiction writers." As we watch, Emily walks over to Samir, or, should I say *floats,* because that's more like it, as her feet barely touching the ground. And when she gets in front of Samir, she plunges her hand right through his stomach, wiggling her fingers on the other side.

"Ack!" Samir sputters. "You *are* a g-g-g- . . ." He doesn't finish. Instead, his eyes roll back in his head and he faints. Hana catches him. Emily Brontë withdraws her hand, showing that Samir wasn't harmed.

"Okay, I stand corrected," Hana says, stooping and slapping Samir on the face. He comes to sounding groggy and out of it.

"Oh, do me next! Do me!" Blade says, gleefully clapping her hands together. She's in Goth heaven at the moment.

While I'm having a hard time processing this, I do know one thing: I don't like Emily. I don't like the fact that she scared Samir, and I don't like that's she's trapped Ms. W in a book, either.

"Did you have something to do with Kate Shaw's disappearance?" I ask her, suddenly wary. "Do you know where she is?"

"Why, look for yourself," she says, and she tosses me a copy of *Wuthering Heights.* It's old, and the cover is tattered, and when I open it up the title page has a handprint pressing out of it. It looks like someone trying to get out.

"Aaaah," I say, and drop the book.

"Pick it up," Emily commands.

"No," I say, completely freaked out at this point. I have no idea what's going on, but I don't like it.

"Where's my missing page? Page 139?" she asks me. I assume she means the one Coach H took.

"I don't have it," I say, which is true. I stoop and grab the books Ms. W and Coach H were trapped in. I notice they're *Mrs. Dalloway* and *For Whom the Bell Tolls.*

"Put those down. Immediately!" commands Emily Brontë. She's suddenly unnerved now.

"No," I say, clutching the books to my chest.

"You *are* as stubborn as Cathy," Emily says, shaking her head. "I was hoping to do this the easy way, but if you want to be difficult, you'll just have to see for yourself what consequences that brings."

She pulls from her apron a copy of *Dracula.* She opens it and begins to read from it. As she reads, green mist begins seeping out.

"What is that?" I ask.

"Bad news," Blade says, as the spiral of mist continues weaving its way out. As we watch, the mist grows, taking on the shape of a man. And then, suddenly, instead of mist, I find myself staring at a guy, dressed entirely in black from head to toe. His eyes seem to glow red in the light. Mist Man.

"Is that . . . ?" Samir asks.

"Dracula," Blade finishes for him. "I told you, but you didn't believe me."

As if to prove the truth of this, Mist Man gives us a slow, determined smile, showing off his fangs.

Okay, this would be a really good time for a *Scooby-Doo* moment. You know, like the ones where they rip the mask off the monster/ghost/pirate and it turns out to be a prickly old gardener trying to scare people off so he could sell the land to amusement park developers.

I'm getting the feeling, though, based on the look on Dracula's face, that he's not some gardener looking for a get-rich-quick real-estate scheme. And he's also blocking our only exit out of the sitting room: the door.

"There's your Mina," Emily says, pointing to Blade. "Get her. Get them all."

Dracula hisses and takes a step toward us.

"Run," Blade whispers.

Twenty-two

I don't need to be told twice. I may not be an athlete, but I'm not going to wait to get my blood sucked out by the D Man. I can take a hint.

Dracula is guarding the only door, but there is an iron spiral staircase near me that leads up to a kind of loft, running the entire length of the greenhouse. It's a narrow loft, with a metal grate path as a floor, and rows of plants along its one solid wall.

Samir and Hana are already on the staircase. Blade follows and I scamper up after her, losing my footing once and banging my shin hard against the metal step, nearly dropping the books in my arms. I barely even feel it. Dracula grabs my foot, a surprisingly strong grip. I scream and Blade grabs my hand, tugging hard.

"Let her go," she shouts. Hana and Samir also turn and grab Blade, helping her hold on to me.

Blade digs around in her pocket and comes out with a small coin. She throws it at Dracula. It hits him in the forehead, leaving a red burn mark. He hisses, lets me go, and grabs his forehead.

"What was that?" I shout, scurrying up the stairs.

"It was a souvenir coin from the Vatican," she says. "My grandma went last year and brought them back. It was blessed by the Pope. I always carry a few just in case."

I am suddenly very glad she is such an occult freak.

"That works," I say, scrambling after them. The grate we're running on isn't exactly in top shape. It's rusted through in some places and creaks under our weight. I step on what looks like sheet music. It's from *Little Shop of Horrors.* This can't be good.

"Is this going to hold us?" Samir asks.

"Do we have a choice?" I say, as we run.

Ahead of us, I see more of those biting plants. But they're bigger. Much bigger than the one downstairs. These are like mini trees.

"Not more of these," Blade shouts. They lean out and snap at Hana. Samir picks up a hoe leaning against the wall and smacks one. The others start snapping at us, as well, as we barely squeeze by. One of them bites at Blade and manages to snag her skirt. I try to help her get free, but it's got a strong hold. Samir hits it with the hoe, just as another one, the size of a small hatchback, comes to life behind it, lunging for my head and just missing, its plant jaws snapping at air.

We survive the row of man-eating plants just in time

to see a giant bat flap its wings and appear in front of us. It transforms into Dracula.

"Ack!" I cry, coming to a sudden stop, causing Samir, Hana, and Blade behind me to run into me.

Dracula takes a step toward us. A slow step.

"We're in trouble guys," Blade says. This is an understatement. We're stuck with Dracula in front of us and a giant *Little Shop of Horrors* plant behind us, with nowhere to go.

"Do we want to be eaten by plants . . . or eaten by Dracula?" Samir asks.

"At least things can't get worse," Hana says.

We squeeze together tightly and that's when a weak bolt on the grate below us pops loose with a *ping*. The left half of the grate beneath our feet comes loose, causing us to lurch violently to the left, then forward, toward Dracula. I clutch at the railing on the right.

"Thanks for jinxing us," Blade says.

The right bolt gives way then, and we're in a free fall. I scream, grabbing hold of the grate as it swings loose. Our section clangs to a stop at a hard right angle, the bump sending me loose from the grate. I scramble and clutch at air, managing to grab hold of the edge of the railing.

Below me, there's a sheer drop of about thirty feet to the concrete ground below.

I look up and see that Hana and Samir have managed to hop safely over to the stable part of the grate and they're helping Blade up, too. There's now a three-foot gap between them and Dracula.

"Come on," Samir says, laying down and stretching his arm out to me. "Climb!" he commands. I try to climb, using my hands, but there's nothing for my feet to latch on to and the grate is swinging back and forth, making it even harder to hold on. I've lost the books I was carrying and they fall down to the floor below, hitting it with a *thunk*. One lands in such a way that its cover flies open.

"Wow—look—Coach H!" Hana says, and I glance down just in time to see Coach H appear, fully formed, out from his open book. He stoops down and opens the other and Ms. W springs from it. They both look up at once.

"I've got to get the book," Ms. W says, and then she turns back toward the sitting room.

"Hang on!" Coach H shouts, running toward the stairs. "Samir! Help her!"

"I'm trying," Samir grunts, leaning farther down to try to reach me. "Hold my feet!" he shouts at Hana and Blade.

"I can't hold on much longer," I cry. My fingers have gone numb. I can't feel them anymore. Above me, I see Dracula melt into mist again. Now is my chance.

I reach up with one hand and swipe at Samir's. I'm two inches away from him. But then, another bolt in the grate gives way, causing a jolt that is just enough to make me miss Samir and loose my grip entirely on the grate.

The next thing I know, I'm falling.

I don't know if I scream, but I feel the wind completely sucked out of me. I'm falling, arms and legs flailing, and I brace for the thud of impact. Instead, a green mist surrounds me and holds me up, putting me gently on the ground.

For a split second, I feel relief. And then I realize Dracula saved me. And that is not a good thing.

He materializes then with his arms around me. There's no place to go. He pushes my head hard to the side with one hand, exposing my neck, and he opens his mouth wide, showing his sharp fangs.

I squeeze my eyes shut, hoping it won't hurt as bad as I think it will, and I think: *Well, I hope my parents are happy now. I am about to be eaten by the Big Daddy of All Vampires.*

The next thing I know, he's released me and I'm on the ground coughing and rubbing my neck. When I turn over, I see Heathcliff, who is taller than Dracula and much broader, and he has him in some kind of sleeper hold and the two of them are struggling. And just when it looks like Heathcliff might have the upperhand, Dracula disintegrates, changing shape again, this time into dozens of rats, which run over the ground and over me, their little feet hard and scratchy. Heathcliff leaps on several rats, crushing them under the heel of his boot. I can hear the scream of their death throes, loud and shrieking.

I have never been so glad to see Heathcliff. He extends his hand to help me up; I grab it as the rats scurry away.

"What took you so long?" I joke. He gives me a rueful smile.

"Get away from him!" shouts Coach H, who has abandoned the stairs and is headed toward us.

Heathcliff scowls at Coach H, his grip on my hand tightening as he pulls me behind him for protection.

"Behind you!" shouts Ms. W, reappearing with a book in her hands. And not just any book—Bram Stoker's *Dracula*. I get it. She's going to suck him back into the book. She must have gotten it from Emily Brontë, although I don't see her now. She must've gotten away somehow.

Behind me, Dracula has formed again into a man and he's two feet away. Heathcliff whirls, pushing me out of the way. I stumble but catch myself, and it's Heathcliff who takes Dracula head on. Dracula is snapping at him with his jaws and hissing, but Heathcliff is twisting him away, trying to keep his own neck away from Dracula.

Ms. W tosses the book to Coach H, and he attempts to open it and trap Dracula, but Dracula hurls him straight up into the air and the book goes flying off, landing somewhere between me and Ms. W. Coach lands on top of the grating above our heads, and then while I watch, Coach H is literally snatched out of the air by the giant, man-eating plant, chomped on and then swallowed—whole.

Ugh.

Samir shouts and Hana covers her face.

Before I can even register what's happened, Ms. W cries, "Miranda! Look out." Before I know what's happening, Dracula swoops toward me, faster than a wolf. He has me by the throat and he drags me backward, effortlessly, while I clutch at his hand, trying to get it to relax enough so I can breathe. His grip is like steel.

"Let her go!" shouts Ms. W, who has once again picked up the copy of Bram Stoker's *Dracula*. It's in her hands and glowing bright red.

Dracula turns, scowls, and drops me, turning into a wolf. He gallops over and knocks her flat on her back, the book flying straight out of her hands.

"Ms. W!" I shout, as the wolf stands on Ms. W's chest, snarling and drooling, getting ready to bite. She struggles with the wolf's jaws and I notice that her entire dress is soaking wet. It's like she just fell into a pool.

And then, as I watch, Ms. W disappears. Or, rather, she sinks straight into the solid concrete ground, leaving nothing but a puddle of water.

At first I think Dracula caused it, but the wolf looks just as confused as I am, sniffing at the ground where Ms. W used to be and whining. Then, in another second, she comes back up through the ground, behind the wolf, snatches up the book, and opens the cover.

She starts reading a scene from the end of the book— the last sentence of the book—and then as I watch, Dracula is drawn into it as if it's a kind of black hole. He struggles, changing shape as he goes, first into a bat, then mist, and finally into his human form, but the book won't be denied. After the last bit of him is sucked back into the book, Ms. W shuts the cover with a hard snap, trapping him inside.

Stunned and surprised, all I can do is stare with my mouth open. Heathcliff picks himself up from the ground and dusts himself off.

"Now it's your turn," Ms. W tells Heathcliff. As I watch, she takes a copy of *Wuthering Heights* out of her pocket. It's at that moment that I really understand completely for the first time that Heathcliff = *the* Heathcliff. He's no poser. He's the actual character from the book. Ms. W means to suck Heathcliff back into *Wuthering Heights*. Heathcliff is frowning at Ms. W, but doesn't move.

"No!" I shout, suddenly on my feet and standing protectively in front of Heathcliff. He may be many things, but he doesn't deserve to be sucked back into some dusty volume. He's saved my life now at least three times. Without him, I'd be dead long ago. Not to mention, he just fought off Dracula to save me.

"Move aside, Ms. Tate," Ms. W commands.

"No. You can't do this. Not yet," I say.

That's all the delay Heathcliff needs. He leaps in front of me, pushes Ms. W off balance, and whips the copy of *Wuthering Heights* straight out of her hands. In an instant, he disappears out the side door of the greenhouse.

Ms. W steadies herself against the wall, still dripping wet, and shakes her head. "You may have just killed yourself," she tells me cryptically as she sets her mouth in a thin line.

"What do you mean? And what is going on around here?" I shout. "Who the hell are you?"

"I am Virginia Woolf," she says. "The writer. I drowned myself in a river in 1941."

Twenty-three

First Emily Brontë? And now Virginia Woolf?

"Okay, who *isn't* a ghost around here?" I ask.

"That's an excellent question," say Samir above our heads. "But before you answer that, we could use a little help."

He's standing with Blade and Hana and still trapped on the railing between the gap and the giant snapping plant that just ate Coach H. The three of them are barely fighting off the giant plant.

"You know, no hurry or anything," Hana says, as she fights back the plant with a rake, only to have it bite off the end and eat it.

The plant starts shaking suddenly and then, I swear, belches. First, it belches up the rake head, which comes flying down from the top of the greenhouse, hitting the floor with a *clang*. And then, in one great convulsion, Coach H claws his way out of the plant. Once outside, he gives it a great punch on the jaw. It rears back and then goes limp.

"God, I hate flowers," he says, wiping bits of plant goo off his shoulders. "Ms. Woolf is telling the truth," he adds. "She is *the* Virginia Woolf."

"So if she's Virginia Woolf, who are you?" Hana asks.

"Ernest Hemingway," he says, flicking off more goo.

"Okay, who *isn't* dead around here, raise your hand," Samir says, and he puts his hand in the air.

"Oh my God. This is so cool," Blade says.

I like to think of myself as a reasonable person (reasonable = NOT crazy). I have just seen Dracula come to life and now my teachers are *famous dead people?*

"So let me get this straight," I say. "You're *the* Ernest Hemingway. As in *For Whom the Bell Tolls?*"

"Among others," he says.

"You wrote the book that the movie with Sandra Bullock and Chris O'Donnell were in. What was it?"

"In Love and War," Coach H sighs, sounding weary.

"And you're Virgina Woolf. Nicole Kidman played you in *The Hours*. She doesn't really look anything like you, you know."

"Thanks for that," she says. "And if you keep quoting our work from movies, I'm going to have to flunk you for the semester."

Touchy.

"Wait a second," Samir says. "Where's Ashton Kutcher? We're all being punk'd, right? This is just all a big joke, isn't it?"

Coach shakes his head. "Sorry, no joke," he says.

"Wait—that's why the buildings are all so cold," Blade says suddenly. "Because you guys are ghosts!"

"Yes," Coach says, nodding.

"And why your faces don't show up in any of the yearbook pictures," I add.

"That's right," Ms. W says.

"And the flickering lights on campus," Hana adds.

"Yep, guilty," Coach H says.

"Are there more of you?" Samir asks.

Ms. W nods. "The entire Bard faculty," she says. "And the Guardians, too, although they aren't writers. They come from all backgrounds."

"I am *so* going to ask for my tuition back," Samir says. "When my dad hears about this, he is going to *flip.*"

"Here's the thing," Ms. W says. "You can't tell them."

"First of all, they'd never believe you," Coach H says. "And second, you can't actually tell them. It's impossible."

"What do you mean, impossible?"

"If you try talking about the school, or specifically about us, outside the campus grounds, you can't," Ms. W tells us. "To anyone not on this island, you won't be able to make the words come out of your mouth. You won't even be able to say our names."

"We could make you come with us—to prove it," I say.

"You can't make us do anything," Coach H says.

"But even if we wanted to go with you, we couldn't. We're trapped on this island. We can't leave."

"This place is cursed, isn't it?" Blade says, sounding really excited. "This is SO cool."

"Not cursed, exactly," Coach says.

"It's purgatory. For you and for us," Ms. W says. "Only we're dead, so we get to spend a lot longer here than you do."

"But I don't understand," I say. "Isn't there supposed to be heaven and hell? Or reincarnation? Or something?"

"We're here because we died before our time," Coach H says. "We left tasks uncompleted in our life and so we have to pay for that, spiritually, here, before we're released. To go to the next plane. Whether that's heaven or hell or another life, I can't tell you."

"So do you know what it is you were supposed to do?"

"I was supposed to write another three novels," Ms. W says. "But I drowned myself in a river near my home first."

"You drowned yourself?"

"Just like Ophelia," she says. When I have a blank look on my face, she sighs and shakes her head. "Hamlet's girlfriend?"

"Sorry, I don't get it," I say.

"Never mind," Ms. W says. "But when we get back to class, I am assigning you some more homework."

"So that explains the water," I say, stepping away from her dripping sleeve.

"The what . . . ? Oh, goodness," she says, looking down at her sleeve. She closes her eyes a moment as if concentrating. Then, just like that, she's dry. "Sometimes, especially if I don't concentrate, a bit of my death creeps into my appearance. It's quite a scarring event for a soul. I don't recommend it."

"Thanks, I wasn't planning on it, though," I say.

If *only* my parents knew about this. I'd be home in a heartbeat. Then again . . . Maybe I haven't kissed my hopes of a scholarship to Princeton good-bye. Tutoring by *the* Ernest Hemingway could only help with my SATs scores, couldn't it?

"This is heartwarming and all," says Blade, sounding impatient, "but would somebody please explain what is up with these books? And why we just spent a half hour being chased by Dracula?"

"The books you saw tonight are no ordinary books," Ms. W says. "They come from a special vault below the library and, as you have seen, they have the power to bring fictional characters to life."

"You see, when a writer creates a story, he or she creates an alternative universe—literally," Coach H says. "These books act like portals, of sorts, to that real world."

"You guys *do* realize how crazy that sounds, right?" Hana asks, but they ignore her.

"Normally, they're kept hidden in our vault beneath the library," Coach H adds, carefully taking *Dracula* out of Blade's hands. "There they are contained and don't have powers. But if they are taken from the vault, then . . ."

"Then Dracula can come suck on my neck," Blade finishes.

"Exactly."

"Is this part of the reform school? Being sucked dry by Dracula? Because if it is, I swear I'll never do anything bad again in my life," Blade says.

"It isn't supposed to happen," Ms. W says. "In fact, the characters can only come through to this world if they have anchors. People in this world that they can bond with or recognize from their own worlds."

"You mean that we *look* like characters in the books they're from and that's why they follow us around?" I ask.

"That's right," Coach H says. "You're Cathy from *Wuthering Heights.* And your roommate looks like Lucy from *Dracula.* And Hana does look a bit like the heroine of *Jane Eyre.*"

"But why not just destroy all the books, if they're so dangerous?" I ask them.

"We can't. Each of us is linked to one book," Ms. W says. "Our souls are kept there."

"Destroy them, and you destroy us," Coach H finishes.

I suddenly remember page 139 from *Wuthering Heights*. "So that's why you were so upset about the page from *Wuthering Heights*," I say. "It was from one of these special books."

"Now you're catching on," Coach H says.

"Is this the first time books have gotten out?" I ask.

"No," Ms. W says. "The last time this happened was fifteen years ago."

"When Kate Shaw disappeared," I say. "Because she looks like me. And we both look like Catherine."

"That's right."

"So why is Emily doing this?"

Before Ms. W can answer, we're interrupted by the sudden appearance of Headmaster B, who materializes in the room by walking through a wall, and floating above our heads.

"Just when were you two going to tell me my sister was causing trouble—again?" she asks Ms. W and Coach H, who look sort of sheepish.

"Whoa—cool," Blade exclaims, watching Headmaster B float down to the ground in front of us. She has died and gone to occult heaven right now.

"Charlotte, we didn't think there was time," Ms. W says.

"We thought we could handle it," Coach adds.

"Oh yes, four students nearly killed and Heathcliff escaping with *Wuthering Heights*," Headmaster B says. "Congratulations on your handling of the situation. Commendable."

"She really seems pissed," Samir whispers to me.

"B stands for Brontë, doesn't it? You're Charlotte Brontë," I say, suddenly, putting the pieces together. Emily—author of *Wuthering Heights*. Charlotte—author of *Jane Eyre*.

She frowns at me, but she doesn't deny it.

"Enough," Charlotte Brontë snaps. "All of you need to come to my office. Now."

Twenty-four

On the way back to Headmaster B's office, Coach H takes out a cigarette and lights it.

"You know those are bad for you," I tell him, waving off the smoke.

"I'm dead, what else can they do to me?" Coach H digs into his pocket for the silver flask I always see him with. "Want some?" he asks me.

"I'm not supposed to drink," I say. "I'm a minor."

"Oh right, I forgot," he says, putting the flask back in his pocket.

"Teaching isn't really your calling, is it?" I ask him.

"What do you think?" he barks gruffly.

By the time we get to Headmaster B's office, Coach H, Ms. W, and Headmaster B are all arguing among themselves about what happened and what they should do now. They're so wrapped up in talking that they slip right through the wall of the office, leaving the four of us still-living people on the other side of a locked door.

"Uh, guys?" I ask, knocking on the door.

"Hello? We're not dead yet?" Samir says.

After a second, we hear the click of the lock and the door slides open.

"Sorry," Coach H says and lets us in.

I'm still having a very hard time getting used to the idea that my teachers are ghosts. I always knew they were a different species, but I didn't realize they were *dead.*

"We have some questions we need answered," Charlotte says.

"Before I answer anything," I say, "I want to know exactly what happened to Kate Shaw. I think we all do." I look at Hana, Samir, and Blade. They all nod in unison.

Ms. W and Coach H glance over at Charlotte. Her mouth sets in a thin line. She doesn't want to tell us, but she also sees that she doesn't have a choice.

She lets out a long sigh.

"First, you should understand Emily's role in this," Charlotte begins. "Emily had a tenuous grasp on reality when we were living. You see, our mother died when we were both very young and our father didn't care for children. And to escape this reality, she and our other sister, Anne, created a fantasy world called Gondal. They wrote poems about it and created characters. Emily always had a hard time separating the fantasy from the reality. She wanted to live in her fantasy world. For Emily, her fiction has always been more real to her than life itself."

Charlotte looks sad when she says this. She sits down behind her desk and stares off into the fire. I think back to the greenhouse. She was clearly a bit out of it.

"And now that we're here, my sister lost what little was left of her ability to make sense of the world. She was harmless, though, living in her own world, surrounded by her writing, until about fifteen years ago, when she discovered that she could bring her own characters into this world."

Charlotte looks at me.

"Kate Shaw was Emily's first casualty in manipulating time and space. We don't know what happened to her, but we do know that it's very dangerous to bring together the world of fiction and reality."

"When fictional worlds and the real world collide, bad things happen," Coach H says.

"We only discovered this by accident," Charlotte continues. "In 1847, a student got access to the vault and took *Frankenstein*."

"All hell broke loose," Coach H says.

"It was before my time here, as well as Mr. Hemingway's, but the school burned to the ground," Charlotte says, looking very sad. "Many students died. And we realized then the importance of protecting you from the books in the vault."

"Not to mention the fact that if we destroy one of them, we destroy you," Hana points out.

"That, too," Ms. W says quietly.

I can only imagine the chaos that would ensue if some of the delinquent students around here got wind of the fact that they could eliminate the teachers simply by raiding a book vault. There would be anarchy.

"It's also possible that both worlds can be destroyed," Charlotte says. "The fabric of time and space is very thin and there's a delicate balance between our world and theirs. And while one character seems to be able to pass safely into our world, we believe that if more than one character from the same book should cross over to our world, it would upset the balance of the universe and . . ."

"It could bring on the apocalypse," Ms. W adds.

"Armageddon? Wow—this is SO cool." Blade's eyes are wide in awe. I'm sure the apocalypse would be like the Macy's Thanksgiving Day Parade for her.

"We actually don't know that for sure," Coach H says. "But we don't exactly want to test the theory, either."

We're all silent a moment, digesting this piece of information. It's a lot to process all at once. I'm at a boarding school run by famous ghosts, one of them is insane and wants to bring fictional characters to life, potentially destroying the entire universe. It's a lot to swallow.

But something more is bothering me. "So why is Kate Shaw haunting my room?"

"We don't know. That's what we wanted to ask you," Ms. W says. "We thought you might've been helping Emily."

I shrug. "Not me," I say. "I don't know anything about a vault. So how many books does Emily have out?"

"We don't know exactly."

"And how long do we have? You know, before the world goes bye-bye?" Hana asks.

"We don't know."

"What *do* you know?" Samir asks them.

"That we're dead, smart aleck," Coach H says.

"Boys," chides Ms. W. "Let's get back to the problem at hand, shall we? Now, Miranda, do you know why Heathcliff is fixated on you?"

"He thinks I'm Cathy."

"Oh dear," Ms. W says, looking at Charlotte. "Kate Shaw . . ." She trails off.

"We don't know what happened exactly, but we think Heathcliff was involved in her disappearance," Charlotte says.

I swallow, hard.

"You think Heathcliff *killed* her?" Hana asks, sounding worried.

"We don't know for sure," Ms. W says.

"But Heathcliff doesn't kill anyone in *Wuthering Heights,*" Hana points out.

"Heathcliff is a boy without a moral compass," Charlotte tells me. "He is a hard person with a hard heart. He is capable of anything."

"But in the book he loves Cathy," I say.

"But he also does a lot of bad things to a lot of people," Ms. W says. "And besides, we think that it's possible that if fictional characters and real people form real relationships, it offsets the balance between our dimensions."

"And brings on the apocalypse?" Blade prompts, almost sounding excited. I swear, her obsession with the macabre is getting ridiculous. Hana gives her an evil look.

"We think it's why Kate disappeared," Coach H says. "If she got too close to him, it may have destroyed her. That's why we have to find Heathcliff and send him back where he belongs."

"Along with all the characters who don't belong in this world," Charlotte adds.

"Like Mrs. Rochester," Hana says.

"Exactly," Ms. W says, and nods.

Twenty-five

The three ghosts decide that the best way to approach their new problem is to call a faculty meeting in the library. They take us there, but when I try to take a seat, front and center, Charlotte frowns at me.

"Just what do you think you're doing, Miss Tate? You and the other children cannot be privy to this meeting."

"If I'm Dead Girl Walking, then I think I deserve to hear what you guys are planning to do about it," I say.

"I'm sorry, rules are rules," Charlotte says, then points to the nearby library office. Reluctantly, Samir, Hana, Blade, and I file in.

"You know too much as it is," Coach tells us.

"This is for your own safety," Ms. W adds before she closes the door. "We've told you enough of our secrets already. Besides, if you know our plan, then you'll be at risk, especially if Emily thinks she can kidnap you to find out."

"But I can help—" I say, but she's closes the door on me. The next thing we hear is the sound of the key turning in the lock.

"Wow, I had no idea this school was so freakin' *awesome . . .*" Blade starts.

"Hey, Goth Girl, nobody asked you," Hana says. She's clearly had enough of Blade.

"Listen, let's not fight, okay?" I say, trying to barter a truce.

"I still can't believe Emily Brontë violated me like that," Samir says, patting his stomach. "I feel like I was raped."

"I wish she'd done that to me," Blade says in a dreamy, far-off voice. She is seriously disturbed. Hana makes a move toward Blade and I step quickly between them and put a cautioning hand on Hana's arm.

"Get her away from me or I am going to hit her," Hana whispers to me through gritted teeth.

"Guys, let's focus here, okay? We've got to figure out what we're going to do," I say.

"Do? I'm not doing anything," Samir says, sitting down and crossing his arms. "Let our famous goblin friends figure it out. I'm done."

"Technically, they are ghosts, not goblins," Blade says. "Goblins are like evil faeries, but they're about the size of dwarves."

"How do you *know* that?" Samir asks, looking at her for the first time with a kind of fear. "I mean, how does this girl know this stuff?"

"Miranda . . ." Hana warns me. She really wants to deck Blade, I can tell.

"Can we not talk about the occult for five seconds?" I ask, trying to change the subject. "I'm talking about how we're going to get out of here."

"I don't see why we should," Samir says. "We're safe here. I don't see any Draculas or Heathcliffs or Frankensteins, or man-eating plants, or God knows what else. If it's all the same to you, I'd rather just stay, thanks."

"You're just chicken," Blade says.

"That's right. I am, and I'm proud of it," he says. "It means I have half a brain, okay? I've seen enough strange things today to last me a lifetime, thanks."

"I hate to say this, but I think I agree with Samir," Hana says. "I mean, even if we could get out, which we can't, what are we supposed to do?"

"I don't know," I say. "I just feel so helpless sitting here."

"At least we have a good window seat," Samir says.

It's true. One solid wall of the office is a window and it looks right out on the library, where the faculty are gathering. It's not like we could do much and get away with it. We're pretty much in a glass cage.

"Hey, look," Samir says, pointing out at the faculty. "I see dead people."

"Ugh," Hana groans. "That's not funny."

"I still can't believe they're ghosts," I say, watching as they take their seats in chairs around the library tables as Charlotte calls the meeting to order.

They look so real. You know, aside from the fashion disasters most of them are wearing. But I suppose it might be hard to keep up with fashion trends *if you're dead*.

"But are they all famous? I don't recognize all of them," Hana says.

"I think that's part of their punishment," Samir says. "Can you imagine? Dying as a famous author in your time and then winding up at a reform school where half your students have never heard of you? That's got to be a serious blow to the ego, you know?"

"Who do you think Ms. S is?" I ask, watching my klutzy chemistry teacher trip over a snag in the rug as she tries to pull a chair out from the table. She's by far the worst science teacher I've ever had.

"That's easy," Blade says. "That's Mary Shelley. You know, she wrote *Frankenstein*?"

"How do you know that?" Samir asks. "What are you? The Horror Encyclopedia?"

"You guys haven't read *Frankenstein*? I mean, I've read all the horror classics—duh," Blade says, as if we're all morons.

"And him?" I ask, pointing to the bus driver.

"Hunter S. Thompson," Samir says. We all stare at him as if he's insane. "What? I can actually *know* something. I mean, guys, it's obvious. Doesn't he look exactly like the guy Johnny Depp played in *Fear and Loathing in Las Vegas*?"

"You think Hemingway would write me a recommendation to Yale?" Hana asks.

Before any of us can answer, laughter floats up to us through the heating grate in the floor.

"Please tell me that one of you just laughed," Samir says.

The rest of us shake our heads.

"Just so I'm straight here, that crazy laughter is Mrs. Rochester, the crazy nineteenth-century pyromaniac?"

"Don't forget that she could destroy our universe as we know it," Hana adds.

"Boy, I am having a *bad* day," Samir says.

"Do you smell smoke?" Blade says. "I smell smoke."

"Of course you smell smoke," Samir says. "Where there's laughter, there's fire around here."

"I don't suppose anyone has a magical copy of *Jane Eyre* with them?" I ask.

Samir and Hana shake their heads. Blade frowns at me.

"I just thought I'd ask," I say.

Smoke starts seeping into our locked office room from the grate in the floor.

"Uh, guys, we have a little bit of a problem," I say, looking at the grate. The rest of them follow my gaze.

"You call that a little problem?" Samir asks me.

"Compared to Dracula, it's a little problem," I point out. "Words, by the way, I'd never thought I'd actually say out loud."

"Welcome to Bard Academy," Hana says, whipping off her blazer and covering the grate where the smoke is seeping in.

Samir tries the second door of the room, the side door, but it's locked, too. He rams the door with his shoulder, but it doesn't budge.

"Ow," he says, rubbing his shoulder. "That really hurt."

It becomes clear that we're all in big trouble. We're locked inside a tiny office with one sealed window and two doors—one leading back to the library and one leading outside the building—both of which are locked. The smoke is getting thicker. We're all going to die of smoke inhalation if we don't get out of here, and soon.

Blade and I press our faces to the glass and try to get someone's attention, but the faculty members are all fixated on Headmaster B. Blade and I start pounding on the window and shouting, but it seems to be sound-proof because nobody looks in our direction. None of them seem to notice me flailing my arms, either. Wow, for ghosts, they have lousy peripheral vision.

Blade starts to cough. I wave my hand in front of my face, but it does no good—there's too much smoke. I kick at the window, hoping it'll break, but all I get is a sore toe.

"Move!" Samir says. He's got a chair in his hands. He rams it into the window like a battering ram, but it doesn't even make a scratch, and the impact throws him backward. "What the hell is that made out of? Bulletproof glass?"

Now all four of us start shouting and banging at the window, trying to get someone's attention, but the smoke is filling the room quickly and it's getting harder to see.

That's when I see Mrs. Rochester run through the library with a lit torch, screaming and setting fires as she goes. She causes instant mass confusion as some faculty try to catch her and others run off to put out the fires she's setting to books, tables, and the floor.

"For a small woman, she causes a lot of trouble," I say.

"Why can't they catch her?" Samir asks. "They're ghosts, for goodness sake. Why aren't they flying?"

"Why don't they *see* us?" Hana shouts.

The side door in our office rattles. It's the one leading to the outside and it sounds like someone's trying to get in.

"Help," I shout, to the door. "Help us! There's a fire! We're trapped!"

Samir and Blade start shouting, too. And Hana pounds on the door.

There's a hard thud on the door, sounding like someone is throwing their weight into it.

"Wait a minute," Samir says suddenly. "How do we know who that is on the other side? What if it's Dracula?"

"Dracula was sucked back in the book, remember?" I say.

"And I don't think he uses doors," Blade says.

"But what if . . . ?"

Before he can finish his sentence, the door comes

down with a crash and Heathcliff stalks in. He's just kicked down the door.

". . . it's Heathcliff," Samir finishes.

With the usual dark scowl on his face, Heathcliff stomps straight up to me (I suppose if I had to save me as many times as he has, I'd be in a pretty rotten mood, too), scoops me up in his arms, and carries me straight out of the room, leaving Samir, Hana, and Blade to fend for themselves. He's clearly got only one objective: to save me.

"Nice rescue," I hear Hana say, sarcastically, behind me.

I glance back at them and I see that the three of them trot out of the room and start after us, but they all cough and stop, trying to regain their breath. Heathcliff takes me swiftly away from them.

Outside it's morning already and it's light. Off in the distance, I hear the breakfast bell. How did it get so late? I don't have time to dwell on it. I need to get away from Heathcliff. *Now.* He could be a killer for all I know.

"Let me go!" I shout, kicking and squirming in his arms.

Heathcliff contains my squirming easily, carrying me as if I weigh nothing, which I know is not true at all, despite the Bard Academy cafeteria diet.

"Put me down!" I cry, kicking my legs. "Put me down *now.*"

Heathcliff doesn't say a word, just keeps moving. Boy, he's stubborn.

"Let me down! Let me down *now*," I say. I try to punch or hit him, but he's got my arms firmly trapped at my sides.

"Cathy," he says, between gritted teeth. "You know I am no hero of romance. You will not expect from me unlimited indulgences."

"I'm not Cathy!" I shout. "And I know who you are. Who you *really* are. And I know what you did to Kate Shaw. You killed her."

Heathcliff stops in his tracks, standing near the chapel doors. He's taken me this far and now he stops. He looks me in the eye. His eyes are fierce and angry.

"I've not killed anyone," he says. "I may be a villain, but even I have limits. And that sort of villainy I'll leave to the Lintons."

Linton—the name of the man who married Cathy. She died after becoming pregnant with his child. He wasn't a murderer, although in Heathcliff's eyes he was.

"What happened to Kate?"

"You mean Cathy," Heathcliff says. "Kate Shaw was my Cathy's alias. It allowed her free access to the campus."

So, Kate Shaw wasn't a Bard student at all. She was a fictional character. She was Catherine Earnshaw from *Wuthering Heights.*

"She's a character—like you," I exclaim. My mind whirls. Did Coach H, Ms. W, and Charlotte know this? And if so, why didn't they tell me?

Heathcliff looks away from me. "Her life was not in my hands," he says, sounding a little sad. "She went home to Wuthering Heights. It was her choice. She wanted to go."

Heathcliff puts me down now, setting me carefully on my feet. I realize that Heathcliff existing in this plane puts us all at risk, but right now all I see is a sad, misunderstood boy. Someone who spent his life being blamed when no one ever gave him the chance to be anything but the bad guy.

And he doesn't seem capable of destroying the universe. All I know is that he's saved me. Again and again. And I've never properly thanked him.

"Thank you," I say. "For saving my life—again. I don't know how I'm supposed to repay you."

Light from the rising sun shines on us and Heathcliff delicately pushes a strand of hair from my face. He trails his finger down the side of my cheek. He has a surprisingly gentle touch.

"There's no need to thank me," he says. "My soul is yours to do with as you please."

I am momentarily taken aback. Nobody, especially a boy, has ever said anything like that to me before.

That's when I hear shouting behind us. It's Samir, Blade, and Hana. They've caught up to us on foot and they're yelling.

"Get away from her!" Samir says, and he's wielding a stapler he stole from the library office. Hana and Blade have equally ridiculous weapons. Hana has a hole punch and Blade has a trashcan. It's sweet that they want to rescue me, but none of them are any match for Heathcliff.

"Don't!" I say to them, putting my hands up and stepping between them and Heathcliff. "It's okay. He's not what you think."

"But he's a killer!" Hana shouts.

"He's not. It's okay. Let's all just calm down," I say. I'm actually far more worried for them than for Heathcliff. He could do some serious damage to the three of them if he wanted to.

"That's it, run!" Samir says, looking over my shoulder.

I turn and see that Heathcliff has gone. He's heading toward the cafeteria. He glances at me one last time before he disappears inside the doors.

"Did you see that, ladies? I *totally* scared him off," Samir says, slapping the stapler against his palm.

"You didn't scare him," I say. "Please. As if you could scare off a rabbit."

"I wasn't the one doing the running," Samir says. "So you do the math."

"Where is he?" says Ms. W, appearing behind Samir. She has Guardians with her and Coach H.

"Cafeteria," Hana says, and before I can stop them, Ms. W, Coach H, and the Guardians swarm the cafeteria en masse.

Twenty-six

Without even thinking about it, I run after them.

Hana, Samir, and Blade trot after me, but I'm faster. I burst through the cafeteria doors. It's on the early side for breakfast, but there are a surprising number of students dressed and here already. The cafeteria is nearly a third full, even though most of the students are in line, and not yet sitting.

I see Ms. W and Coach H on the fringes of the students, trying to calmly look for Heathcliff without arousing too much suspicion among the students. The Guardians fan out around the tables, doing the same. I scan the crowd looking for him, but I can't seem to find him either.

"Miranda!" someone calls. I turn to find myself staring at Ryan Kent. He's waving at me and walking toward me. Ryan! I've *completely* forgotten about him. I suddenly feel awful. Last time I left him he was in the infirmary with smoke inhalation—the end of our date—

and I'd gone the whole night and not given him another thought. What kind of person am I?

"Ryan—God, how are you? Are you okay?"

"I woke up in the infirmary about an hour ago with a raging headache. Nobody was around, so I just got up and walked here," he says. "How about you? I was worried about you. I couldn't find you and the last thing I remember was leaving you on the stairs."

Poor Ryan. He really does look worried. And why wouldn't he be? Our date ended in a raging fire and me fainting.

"I'm fine. Really—it's just been a crazy night."

"What's happened?" he asks, perplexed.

I blink at him, not sure where to start. The ghost faculty? Dracula? Heathcliff? None of it makes any sense. *Oh, hi, Ryan, you're going to think I am completely insane, but the world might end because there are fictional characters running around in our dimension breaking the laws of physics, and by the way, I think you are gorgeous—would you consider taking my virginity?* Yeah, somehow I think it's not going to fly. You have to see it to believe it.

"Long story," I say. I can't help but glance around the cafeteria. I see that Ms. W and Coach H are still on the prowl. Heathcliff isn't in sight. I wonder if I'm relieved or worried. I'm conflicted, that's for sure. Part of me wants him to escape. The other part of me is screaming that it could bring on the end of the world as I know it.

"I can't believe the Bard arsonist crashed our date. But I will make it up to you, I promise," he says. "Fire is just the first date. You should see what I do for the second."

"Um, sorry, what was that?" I'm not quite listening, I have to admit. I'm a little busy here—we're talking potential end-of-the-world-scenario. And *where* is Heathcliff?

"Uh, you seem a little distracted," Ryan says.

"What? Me? Oh no, I'm just . . ."

"Looking for someone?" he asks me.

"No, well, sort of . . ." I trail off just as my eyes fall on Heathcliff. He's standing near a group of students. Actually, girls. . . . In fact, he's talking to . . . *Parker Rodham*?

Ryan's eyes follow mine.

"Do you know him?" he asks me.

"Sort of," I say, wondering what Parker is up to and why Heathcliff is tolerating it. He's not exactly the social type. Unless he likes Parker. I'm not sure why, but that thought annoys me.

Parker sees me watching them and then she leans in and puts her hand on his arm. I swear, she's flirting!

"Parker seems to like him," Ryan says.

I glance at Heathcliff's face, but I can't read it. He's just scowling, as usual. He looks down at his arm, where Parker is touching him, and frowns.

"You know she thinks she's trying to steal your boyfriend," Hana says, coming up behind us.

"Boyfriend?" Ryan echoes, concern on his face.

"He's not my boyfriend," I say, but Ryan looks doubtful. He is watching me watching Heathcliff.

"She's so going to get what she deserves," Hana says. "She doesn't know that she's playing with fire."

It's then that I remember that in *Wuthering Heights* the only thing Heathcliff cares about is Catherine. Everyone else is expendable. If he thinks I'm Catherine, then Hana is right. Parker is in for a rude awakening.

"And we're not the only ones who have noticed him," Samir says, standing beside Hana. That's when I notice that Coach H has seen him. He's headed in that direction. I have to warn Heathcliff. And, I guess, I have to admit that I should warn Parker, too.

And that's when I do something I know I'll regret—aside from helping Parker. I'm going to walk away from Ryan Kent.

"Ryan, I'll be right back," I say, pushing past him and moving between Heathcliff and Coach H, hoping to intercept him.

Heathcliff notices me then and my eyes flick over to Coach H, who's moving in fast. He follows my gaze and nods.

"What are you doing?" Hana hisses at me, coming up quickly behind me. "You're helping him get away."

I look over and see Guardians moving in behind him. He's surrounded.

"Parker!" I shout. "Look out!"

She just looks at me, giving me a smug smile. She

doesn't see the Guardians. She thinks I'm jealous. What an idiot.

My eyes shift back to Heathcliff, who grabs Parker hard by the arm and spins her around so her back is pressed up against his chest. I was right about him. He doesn't care about her. It dawns on me in that instant that he intends to use her as a hostage.

"Told you Parker would get what she deserved," Hana says. "Trying to steal your guy and look what happens!"

At first, Parker is just surprised. Then she seems to take it as some kind of compliment, like he's trying to hug her, but then when it becomes clear he means to take her into the path of four large Guardians she starts resisting. Heathcliff easily brings her along, as if she were nothing more than a small dog. Out in the aisle, he roughly whirls her in front of him and grabs her by the hair. Ouch. She struggles against him in earnest now, because it's become obvious to her what's already obvious to me. He intends to use her as a human shield.

Parker has made a big mistake. Heathcliff is no good boy in bad boy's clothes. He's an OMDB Boy, through and through. The original bad boy since 1847.

"Get back," Healthcliff tells the Guardians, who slow their approach. Parker is seriously squirming now, and calling Heathcliff all kinds of names. He's completely unfazed.

Everyone in the cafeteria now is looking at them and

all chatter has stopped as everyone waits to see what's going to happen. Are the Guardians going to win? Or is Heathcliff? I can tell you right now that most of the kids are rooting for Heathcliff. This is a reform school, after all. Nobody in prison cheers for the guards to win.

Heathcliff inches closer to the front doors of the cafeteria as the Guardians follow him tentatively, their arms up. A few more Guardians come up from behind. They plan to trap him. But Heathcliff sees it all coming. With one quick motion, he shoves Parker hard toward the first set of approaching Guardians. She whirls, off balance, and stumbles into them. One of the Guardians flings her away and tries to lunge at Heathcliff. She falls to the ground, hard, her skirt flying up and revealing the fact that she's wearing pink polka-dotted underwear with Hello Kitty on them. I can't help but snicker a little (yes, I'm a terrible person and I'm probably going to hell, blah, blah, blah, but this is Parker Rodham, remember? I can gloat about her accidental *Girls Gone Wild* moment. It's my right).

Meanwhile, Heathcliff uses the distraction to make his escape. In one swift motion, he jumps *on top of* the edge of a table, leaps straight into the approaching Guardians from the rear, and with a couple of quick and furious blows, he's free of them. He slams open the doors and is free. The two Guardians he bested are on the ground, groaning.

Some of the kids, in awe, start applauding.

Parker, however, is livid. Her face is bright red and

she glares at me as if she wants to kill me with her bare hands. She is so mad, she actually shoves one of her own clones when said clone tries to help her to her feet. She then starts shouting at Coach H, who is trying to calm her down, but she is in full-fledged temper-tantrum mode. There's no calming her down. Eventually, the Guardians have to take her by force back to her dorm. Her clones follow after, as if on a string.

I turn around to look for Ryan, hoping to start up our conversation where we left off, but he's gone.

Twenty-seven

Heathcliff makes good on his escape. He has a knack for disappearing and he eludes the Guardians with ease.

"If you insist on helping him, I don't know what we're going to do with you," Ms. W says to me, looking very disappointed as we walk back to the dorm. Hana and Blade are with us, but Samir and Coach H have headed back to Macduff, the junior/senior boys' dorm.

"I didn't help," I say.

"You did, and lying doesn't improve matters," Ms. W says. "I don't know how much clearer I can make this. He doesn't belong in this world, Miranda."

"But you said yourself you don't know if him being here will really cause the end of the world. You said you don't know exactly, but you think it could."

"Do you really want to take that risk?" Hana asks me. "I mean, I know he's hot and all, but you have to use your brain here."

"He's not hot, is he?"

"Duh," Hana says. "He so obviously has bad boy mojo, and you are *completely* falling for it."

Am I?

"He's only going to end up doing more harm than good," Ms. W says. "Remember Tyler?" she reminds me gently.

It's true. People tried to warn me about Tyler, and I just didn't want to listen. Maybe Ms. W is right about Heathcliff, and I just don't want to see it.

Back at our dorm, Ms. W orders the three of us to go to bed. We're given a full day's pass from Saturday activities—which include mandatory study hall and assembly—and ordered to go straight to our rooms to sleep. I'm so keyed up that I don't think it's possible for me to sleep, but amazingly, I put my head on the pillow and I'm out. I sleep like the dead, probably because I've spent so much time with them. I slip into a dream that's so real, I could swear it's really happening.

In the dream, I'm standing in a graveyard, which under normal circumstances would seem creepy, but here for some reason just seems sad. There's a funeral going on, and everyone is dressed in black, in period clothes—I'd say more than a hundred years old. The crowd around the grave disperses and I see Heathcliff, standing and staring at the grave. As I approach him, I see the name on the gravestone. It says: Catherine Earnshaw Linton.

Heathcliff's true love.

Heathcliff, normally so strong and stoic, drops to his knees and starts sobbing and clawing at the gravestone. My heart breaks watching him. He's in misery.

I put my hand on his shoulder and he looks up at me, then wraps his arms around my legs, sobbing. I'm not sure what to do, I put my hand on his head to try to comfort him.

That's when, out of nowhere, Emily Brontë, the raving woman in the black dress, appears before us. She lifts her hands and the ground beneath our feet gives way. Heathcliff and I are both falling, tumbling, straight into Catherine's grave.

I wake with a start, cold sweat dripping down my back.

The dim light of morning is shining through my window and it takes me a moment to realize that I've slept the entire day and all night. I guess this is what happens when you don't sleep for a month and then are up all night.

I rub my face to try to wake myself up from the nightmare. What could it mean? I can't help but think that Heathcliff isn't the dangerous one. Emily Brontë is.

Everything from the night before (or night before that, technically) comes rushing back to me. Was it real? Or was it all a dream? Ghost teachers of the literary variety, fiction coming to life. That's when I notice on my bedspread, lying across my feet, there's the page from *Wuthering Heights*. The one Kate Shaw had hidden in her closet.

I just stare at it. Where did it come from? Coach H took it ages ago and now here it is, back on my bed?

I glance around my room, but Blade's bed is empty. She must've gotten up a long time ago. Tentatively, I pick up the page. I hold it like it might be dynamite. I don't know what kind of powers it has, or whether just holding it might bring about the end of the world.

I look at the page; I hadn't really read it carefully before, but it's the scene between Heathcliff and Catherine when Catherine is dying (has made herself sick because Heathcliff and her husband Linton can't get along), and Heathcliff is accusing her of betraying him by marrying someone who isn't her true love. It's a heart-wrenching scene.

I turn it over and that's when I see handwriting. *Kate's* handwriting.

It says, "You are in danger."

"Kate? Cathy? Whoever you are. Is that you?" I say to the room. "If you're there, I need some help. What should I do? How am I in danger?"

The room is silent. No closet lights go on. No drawers open. I can't tell if she's here or not and I'm starting to feel a little silly that I talked to an empty room. Besides, she wasn't even a real girl, so how could she be a ghost?

Reluctantly, I pull myself from bed and get dressed. I decide to put the page from *Wuthering Heights* in my pocket and try to give it to Ms. W or Coach H. They ought to have it back.

I wander into the dorm's den, looking for Ms. W, and find her directing a large group of students lingering in the hall in a line that looks like they're waiting for concert tickets to go on sale. Some are leaning against the wall and others are sitting on the floor in the hall. I push my way to the front and see something even stranger than ghosts.

Payphones have appeared in the den. Five of them. They weren't there before and now they are. They are the kind of payphones Clark Kent would use to change into his Superman outfit, big glass-and-wood boxes with folding doors for privacy.

Where did they come from?

They all have girls inside, talking on the phone. And I just thought I'd seen it all on this campus.

Ms. W is standing by them, navigating the wait, summoning girls up to use the phones.

"What's going on?" I ask her.

"Haven't you read your campus mail? Today is parents' Sunday. The only time you get to talk to your family before Thanksgiving."

And then I remember. Last week, the flyer in my mailbox. The one that said we can make two outgoing calls and that our parents have been notified to be on alert for our calls.

I was supposed to write up something to say to Dad, too, but I guess I've been a little busy. I remember suddenly the half-written letters that I've been writing to him. I never managed to finish one.

"How are you doing this morning?" Ms. W asks me, looking concerned.

"As good as can be expected, considering." Considering I was almost eaten by a plant, sucked dry by Dracula, burned by Mrs. Rochester, and abducted by Heathcliff.

As I watch, a girl exits one of the phone booths. Ms. W signals to me.

"Go on," she tells me. "You're next."

"Hey! No fair," cries Parker Rodham, who is sitting near the fireplace with her clones. "We've been waiting for an hour."

Ms. W sends Parker a look that silences her immediately.

"But, Ms. W . . ." I start, trying to tell her about the wayward book page. She silences me with a wave of her hand.

"Come on, Miranda," Ms. W says, waving me forward. "Alexander Graham Bell won't wait for you all day."

"Do we really have time for this now?" I ask Ms. W, thinking that there are clearly bigger problems I need to deal with than talking to my parents. Saving the world, for starters.

"The world will wait," Ms. W says, as if reading my mind. "For your family, you need to make time."

Reluctantly, I step into the phone booth, half expecting to see the inventor of the telephone sitting there. But it's empty.

"You won't be able to tell them about Bard," Ms. W cautions. "What happens here, stays here."

"Just like Las Vegas," I say, but Ms. W doesn't get the joke.

I dial my mom's number and Lindsay picks up on the second ring.

"Oh, it's *you*," she says, sounding disappointed. "I thought you were going to be a telemarketer. I was going to mess with you."

That's my sister for you. She'd rather talk to a telemarketer than me.

Lindsay's favorite thing next to watching the Discovery Channel is to get up the hopes of telemarketers by promising to buy what they're selling and then at the end of the conversation, admit that she's only thirteen. Lindsay has no real friends, so she has to resort to taunting telemarketers. It's sad, really.

"So I can see you miss me a lot," I say sarcastically. "So? What have I missed?"

"You mean aside from me wearing all your shoes?"

"I'm not going to dignify that with an answer," I say.

"Well, for one thing, you missed *big* news."

"What? Did Dad get divorced—again?"

"No, silly, that wouldn't be news," Lindsay says, and I have to laugh. "No, Mom went on a date."

"What? Mom doesn't have a social life."

"You mean she *used* to not have one," Lindsay says. "She's gone out on *three* dates now with my math teacher, Mr. Perkins. I *totally* set them up. It's, like, so cool. I'm totally gonna get an A this semester."

Oh my God. I leave the house for a month and Mom has gone insane. She's going on a date with Mr. Perkins? He wears short-sleeved polyester shirts and his pants only come down to his ankles. He's not fit to date!

"Miranda? Oh Miranda, is that you?" Mom cries, picking up the phone and butting into our phone conversation. "Oh dear, how are you? Are you okay? I've been trying to call, but the school administrators have said we can't talk to you during your adjustment period. I've been getting your letters. Have you gotten mine?"

Normally, I'm annoyed by Mom's drama, but it's nice to hear that she misses me. And for once, I'm not annoyed when she spends twenty minutes out of thirty talking about how she's considering liposuction.

I feel like I've grown up a lot in the last month. I find that I'm not even mad at her anymore for sending me away. All I feel is longing to see her and Lindsay. Hearing their voices makes me homesick.

"So what have you been up to at Bard? Have you been studying the classics?"

"Uh, yeah," I say, thinking Mom has no idea how true this is. "They really immerse you in literature here."

I suddenly really want to tell her about the ghosts, and about Kate Shaw, no matter how crazy it sounds, but I find, just as Coach H predicted, that I can't find the words. The more I try to tell them, the more I can't speak. Literally, I'm tongue-tied.

I guess the spell of the school works on phone lines, too. You can't talk about the goings-on at Bard to anyone outside campus.

"Did you develop a stutter or something?" Lindsay asks me, still on the line.

"It's nothing," I say. "Forget it."

Ms. W taps on the glass after a little while.

"Time to call your father," she tells me, tapping her watch.

Reluctantly, I let Mom and Lindsay go, and dial Dad's mobile number. I get his voicemail—of course. I hang up without leaving a message. I have no other choice but to call his house and risk getting Carmen. As the phone rings, I pray she's out shopping or something, which is probably the very first time in history that I've actually *wished* she was out spending my college fund.

On the third ring, Carmen answers.

Dammit.

"Hello? Hello!" she says, sounding annoyed. I've paused too long.

"Um, Carmen, it's me, Miranda."

"Miranda who?" she asks.

Nice one. You see why I'm not fond of calling her "Stepmother," despite Dad's insisting.

"Miranda Tate. Your stepdaughter?"

"Oh," she says, sounding disappointed. As if another Miranda might be more interesting. "Your father isn't here."

Wow. She's ruder to me than most people are to telemarketers. She makes Cinderella's stepmom look like Mother Teresa.

"But didn't he know that today is the only day I can talk to him?" I ask her, trying to keep the disappointment out of my voice, but failing. I mean, the one chance he has to talk to me for three months and he can't wait by the phone for an hour?

"I don't know. He's golfing—as usual," Carmen says, sounding annoyed. "Anyway, I have to go."

"Well, can you tell him—"

I don't get to finish my sentence because Carmen hangs up on me.

"—that I called?" I finish, but it's too late. I'm talking to a dial tone.

Ouch.

I stare at the phone. I can't quite believe what jerks they are. Carmen and my dad both. But, for once, I don't cry. I don't know if dealing with ghosts and the supernatural has empowered me or what, but this doesn't seem like the end of the world like it normally would when Dad ignores me. I mean, you know, now that it's possible the world might *really* end. For once, I see clearly that it's not my fault that Dad is blowing me off. It's *his.* If he doesn't want to know me, I think, *his* loss. There are plenty of people who find me interesting. Heathcliff, for one, and Ryan Kent for another, I think. So if Dad can't be bothered, then he's the jerk. Not me.

Ms. W pats me on the shoulder as I get out of the phone booth. "It's not your fault, you know," she says, as if she heard the entire conversation with Carmen.

"I know," I say, and I really mean it.

"If I could, I would go haunt his house," she whispers to me, and this makes me smile. I imagine Dad trying to deal with ghosts. He can't even deal with his ex-wives or his daughters. I'd like to see him deal with the dead.

Twenty-eight

Ms. W cautions me to be careful walking about on campus, since Emily Brontë and Heathcliff and Mrs. Rochester are still on the loose. She makes me promise that should I see Heathcliff, I will sound the alarm immediately. I promise to do so, even though I'm not quite sure how I feel about that. I check my room for Blade, but it's empty. Hana's room is empty, too. Strange.

I strike out onto campus, still a little surprised that she let me go out at all, with the hope of finding Ryan Kent and apologizing. I can't help but feel like he's got the entirely wrong idea about Heathcliff and me, even though I can't even explain to myself that particular relationship.

I think about Ryan and the look on his face before the fire ruined the moment. Was he going to kiss me? Maybe I'd just been imagining it. Maybe he was just about to tell me I had something on my face—like Fritos crumbs. Then again, I'm pretty sure he was going to kiss me. He had that same look in his eyes that Tyler did when Tyler went in for the sloppy kill, except that Ryan wasn't drunk or belligerent.

But what about Heathcliff? Do I have feelings for him, too?

Life is way too complicated at the moment. I have so much in my head, I don't know what to think.

Outside, the campus is nearly deserted. I guess everyone is inside trying to make phone calls. I guess that goes for Hana and Blade, too, although they weren't in the dorm. It's mid-October and the chill in the air is definite. The wind kicks up, rustling the leaves and making it sound like whispers. Birds settle on the tops of trees and flocks of them fly off in the distance, looking more like bats.

Leaves rustle along the path in front of me, making an eerie sound like footsteps, but every time I turn I see nothing. The campus has the feel of the opening scene in *28 Days Later,* where the guy wakes up in the hospital to a deserted London. I wouldn't be surprised if fast-running, red-eyed zombies started sprinting across the commons.

I find myself standing in front of the boys' dorm, Macduff, wondering how I'm going to find out where Ryan Kent is. The girls aren't allowed in the boys' dorms, just like the boys aren't allowed in the girls'. Not that I'd let that stop me. I try the front door of the dorm, but it's locked.

I peer into one of the windows and see the lounging

room is full of boys waiting to use the phone. I don't see Samir, but I do see Ryan. He makes eye contact with me. I wave at him, but he looks pointedly at me and then away. He doesn't wave. He doesn't even acknowledge me.

My heart sinks.

He's mad at me. He's mad about the whole Heathcliff scene in the cafeteria. I try once more. I tap on the glass, but Ryan just looks up at me again and then turns away, putting his back to me.

Ouch. Rejected.

I step back from the window and stick my hands in my blazer pockets for warmth, and my fingers touch the page of *Wuthering Heights* that I'd put there. With all the family drama, I forgot to give it to Ms. W. I pull it out to look at it and notice that the handwritten message is gone. Huh? How did that happen? It was there, I could've sworn the warning was there, and now it's not.

As I study the page, a gust of wind kicks up, whipping it out of my hands as if someone plucked it from my fingers.

Crap! I lunge after it, but the wind has taken it. I chase it down the path as it rolls and tumbles like a leaf in the wind. Over and over. When I get closer to it, the wind picks up and blows it just out of my reach. If I didn't know better, I'd say the page was leading me somewhere.

The paper just keeps blowing forward, landing, finally on the steps of the library.

As I'm standing there, the library door opens with a

creak, like an invitation. "Kate?" I find myself whispering. "Is that you?"

Is she opening the door? I realize she's a fictional character, but maybe she is also a ghost. At Bard, I suppose anything is possible.

The wind kicks up again and the piece of paper blows inside the library.

I hesitate. I should *not* go inside. I should turn around right now and leave. There's a point in all those horror movies when the girl or guy does something incredibly stupid (goes off separately from the group into the dark woods, for example), and you just want to shout at him to *go back.* The only reasonable course of action is to leave the haunted mental hospital/forest/mansion/town. But do they ever leave the haunted mental hospital/forest/mansion/town? No, they don't. They just stay there like a bunch of morons and get hacked to pieces.

I should turn around, right now, and head back to my dorm.

But I don't.

I need to get that page back.

I walk inside the library and pick up the piece of paper, which is now lying still on the ground.

That's when I look up and see Heathcliff standing on the other side of the library.

He looks at me—sadly almost?—and turns to walk down the aisle.

"Wait . . ." I say, but he doesn't listen to me. He just keeps walking.

I pause. Should I go get a Guardian? But there isn't time. I'm torn. Heathcliff is going to get away if I don't follow. And besides, I think suddenly, maybe I can convince him to turn himself in. I stuff the page in my pocket and chase after him, down the aisle of the library and pause, keeping distance between us, as he reaches into a bookshelf and pulls down a book: *Shakespeare's Complete Works.*

The floor beneath his feet starts to glow, and slowly pieces of the floor start to slide open. It's a door—a door to the vault. As I watch, Heathcliff starts walking down, through the door in the floor, down what must be stairs. He is bathed in an eerie blue glow.

I hesitate. Should I go for help? I feel like there's no time. What if he gets away?

I make a decision to go after him, just as the door starts to close. I make it down part of the stone staircase just as the door closes above my head. The vault is dusty and cobwebbed, because naturally the answers to this mystery have to be in a creepy, dirty basement that smells like mothballs. All it lacks is some bloody handprints and it would be straight out of *The Blair Witch Project.* I mean, seriously. I'm going down here *voluntarily*?

But it's too late to change my mind now. I don't know how to open the door above my head. I see Heathcliff's shadow below me and decide to follow. I'm not sure if he knows I've followed him or not, but he isn't letting on if he knows.

The staircase is winding, so you can't quite see what's around the corner until you're there.

At the bottom, I see an underground library the size and scope of the library above me. The blue glow is coming from lights along the walls. They're like torches, but with blue lights. It's like they're all gas burners or something, except that I smell no gas. This is like no library wing I've ever seen. It's more like a dungeon.

I notice for the first time the books on the shelves. They are old and unraveling just like the ones I saw in the greenhouse. This is *definitely* the vault. The one with the magic books.

I don't see Heathcliff anymore, though. Where did he go?

There are so many aisles that he could've gone down any number of them. I start walking down the main one, looking down either side, down long rows of bookshelves, looking for him.

Down at the far end of the library, there's a sitting room, complete with a fireplace, with the flames going, and in front of it are Samir, Hana, and Blade. They're all tied to chairs and gagged. I rush to them and take off their gags.

"You've got to get out of here," Hana says urgently as I kneel down and try to undo the knots on their wrists.

"It's a trap," Blade adds.

"You can untie us first, though, if you want," Samir says.

"Don't listen to him, Miranda," Hana says. "You need to get out of here. This is a trap. She wants . . ."

The knots are too tight. I can't get them undone. As I struggle with them, I see, out of the corner of my eye, a flash of movement. I struggle with the ropes even faster, trying to get them loose. On the other side of us there's another flash. It's a woman running.

"She's here," Blade says.

"Run," Hana says urgently, but before I can, two ice-cold hands come around my arms. They're like steel.

That's when I hear Emily Brontë's voice in my ear.

"Nice of you to come for a visit, my dear," she says. "Why don't you stay a while?"

Twenty-nine

"Welcome, Miranda," Emily says, as Heathcliff appears beside her. "Bind her," she orders him.

"Wait, what's going on?" I cry, as Heathcliff puts his hands on my shoulders and sits me down in the chair. I send him a pleading look, but he doesn't look me in the eye. He puts my hands behind my back and ties my wrists to the chair.

"Told you it was a trap," Hana says.

"Silence!" Emily calls. Instantly, Hana stops talking.

On the other side of Emily, I see Mrs. Rochester walking up. I squirm and fight the ropes, but it's no use. I'm held fast. I shout as loud as I can, but no one seems fazed.

"We're deep underground and the walls are at least ten feet thick," Hana says. "It's useless."

All I can do is watch, helplessly, as Mrs. Rochester takes up her stance by the fire, staring into it, transfixed. I glance over at Heathcliff. I can't believe I was so wrong about him and everyone else was so right. He lured me here. He was helping Emily Brontë all along.

"The page?" Emily says then, and that's when Heathcliff reaches into my pocket, pulls out the page of *Wuthering Heights,* and hands it over to Emily Brontë.

"You realize that the book didn't work without the missing page," Hana says.

"I was trying to save you guys," I point out.

"Yeah, nice rescue," Samir says, struggling against the ropes. "Next time, you might want to think about bringing reinforcements. You know, just a thought."

"Heathcliff, what are you *doing*?" I cry. "She's crazy. You can't help her. She's going to destroy everything."

Emily takes the page, studies it, and then looks at me. "You're wasting your time," she tells me, surprisingly clear for an insane woman. "I'm his creator, and he cannot stray from my will."

I look up at Heathcliff, but he looks away from me. Is this true? Is he just her pawn?

"Heathcliff," I say. "You can't be helping her. She's insane."

Heathcliff won't look at me.

"Ah, Miranda, you are so like my Cathy," Emily says. "I can see the family resemblance."

"Family resemblance? What are you talking about?" I ask, fighting against the ropes that bind me to the chair.

"Did my sister Charlotte not tell you? That is such a shame," Emily says. "Did you think it was just a coincidence that you looked so much like my Cathy? Like Catherine Linton? The same Catherine that is my dear Heathcliff's love? You are her great granddaughter, five times over."

"That's not possible," I sputter. "She's a fictional character—she doesn't exist."

"That's where you are wrong, my dear," Emily says. "Fifteen years ago was not the first time Cathy—Catherine—crossed over to this world. She'd done so several times before, as did her daughter, Elizabeth."

"But her daughter wasn't named Elizabeth," Hana says. "She was named Catherine. After her mother." Leave it to Hana to know all the details of *Wuthering Heights.*

"That is correct," Emily says. "That was the name of her older daughter. But she had twins, you see. In my version, she had twins, Catherine and Elizabeth. Elizabeth escaped into this world, however, in 1848. She found her anchor in a boy she met at this school. That was Miranda's great-great-great-great-grandfather."

I can't believe what I'm hearing. I mean, I knew there was some Cherokee in my family, but now fictional characters? How is this possible?

"Elizabeth Linton married and had three children, and then she became real in this world and disappeared forever from *Wuthering Heights,*" Emily says. "And now you, her descendant, are the key to making all my characters real."

"I don't understand," I say.

"Your mixed blood gives you a power nobody else has over these books. Over the vault itself. Or didn't my sister tell you that? I guess they didn't want you to know," Emily says. "You are the key to opening the door fully between these dimensions. You span them both, you see."

Hana, Samir, and Blade all look at me.

"That is *way cool*," Blade says.

Emily takes out *Wuthering Heights* and replaces the missing page. As I watch, miraculously, it's fused back to the original spot.

"But what about the ghost? In my room?"

"There was never a ghost in your room," Emily says. "Unless you count me as that ghost. I was playing the part. Leading you around to clues. I wanted to draw you here, so that you could open the portal—permanently. No longer will there be a barrier between these worlds. And Heathcliff, of course, helped me. He'd do anything to be reunited again with his *real* Catherine."

Heathcliff glances up to Emily, and then his eyes rest briefly on me.

"But you do understand that the world will end," I say to Emily.

"It may or may not," she says, "but it's a risk worth taking. Even if the world is destroyed, it means I'll be free from this prison. Now, Miranda, it's time for you to read to us." Emily places the open book on my lap.

"No," I say, shaking my head. "I won't do it."

"Then your friends die now," Emily says. She places

her hands around Samir's neck and squeezes. He struggles.

"Don't hurt him," I shout. "I'll do what you say."

I start to read, and suddenly the walls around us shake. It feels like there's going to be an earthquake. Books fly off the shelves, thudding to the ground. Bits of dust and rock fall from the ceiling as the vault shakes.

Beneath our feet, a giant crack appears in the ground, and a bright, white light shines through it. Our dimension. It's falling apart.

"End-of-the-world time," Blade says.

A hand pops out of the book—a girl's hand. Catherine's, I think, but I'm not sure how I know it's her.

That's when Charlotte comes up through the floor of the room. Her ghost appears, holding her own copy of *Jane Eyre*.

Ms. W and Coach H appear then, too, walking into the room through the vault walls.

"You didn't really think we'd just let Miranda wander around without some protection?" Ms. W says, and then she winks at me. I feel immensely relieved.

Heathcliff stands up, looking from one teacher to another, trying to figure out where he should place his energies.

"Emily, stop this at once," she demands. "You will destroy everything."

"Oh, I hope I do," she says. "I can think of no better way to be released from this prison. This world will be destroyed, yes, but my Moors will live on, with me in them."

"But the world, these students, you would risk killing them all?"

"I would sooner save my dog than any one of these students," Emily says, suddenly sounding bitter. "They're all spoiled, every one of them. They don't know what suffering is. My Heathcliff now is barely nineteen, and he's known a lifetime of suffering."

I look at Heathcliff. Now that I know his current age, I realize he's not *that* much older than me. Four years. It's a lot, but not as much as I thought. In the firelight, he looks even younger. He looks at me.

"I don't understand," Charlotte says.

"I've found a way to *live* in my book, forever," Emily says. "With Heathcliff and Catherine here, I can go inside the book. Live there. Forever."

With that, she puts her own hand into the book and as she does so, the girl's hand changes. It starts to . . . wither. And, just as we watch, the flesh falls away, until nothing is left but the bones beneath.

Heathcliff's face falls.

"What are you doing?" Heathcliff cries.

"Catherine's life for hers," Charlotte says.

Mrs. Rochester seems to come to life suddenly, her eyes fixed on Charlotte. She lunges suddenly for the fire, grabbing a flaming log without caring about its heat, and charges Charlotte. Taken off balance, she drops *Jane Eyre* and struggles with her own character, trying to restrain her. There's an odd tug of war, where Charlotte tries to keep her from setting fire to the pile of books on the floor.

"Get her or we're all destroyed!" Charlotte cries. Ms. W goes to help Charlotte stop Mrs. Rochester, who seems to be intent on burning books, and Coach H approaches Emily, but Heathcliff springs into action, knocking him back. Then, in one swift motion, Heathcliff swipes the book from Emily's hands. It's still open and the skeleton hand is still sticking out of it.

"Hand it here, Heathcliff," commands Emily.

Coach H circles carefully, ready to spring if necessary, but unsure of what Heathcliff plans to do.

"No," I say. "No, don't. Look what she's done already—Catherine is dead. She means to kill us all, so she can live."

Heathcliff looks at me and then at Emily.

"You cannot disobey your creator. Your thoughts and actions have always been mine to control," Emily says. "And this is your fate, Heathcliff. It has always been your fate. To mourn the loss of Catherine. It's what I created you for. Not to love. To mourn."

Ever so gently, he touches the fingers of the skeleton hand. Heathcliff's face settles into a scowl and he slams the book shut. The crack in the floor closes. The building stops shaking. He glares at the fire.

It's as if Emily knows his thoughts already, because she says, "If you destroy that book, you destroy yourself, as well as me. Remember that."

He looks at the book a little longer and then at the fire.

"You are Catherine's murderer," he says. "And you would be still. You would kill her again and again. Why? For your amusement?"

"No," Emily says, shaking her head. "She dies to make your love great. And if you destroy this book, you'll never see her again, not even for a brief time. You'll be dead yourself. Trapped forever away from the things you love."

"I see her now," Heathcliff says, looking at me.

"That is not the true Cathy. She's not your love. And she'll betray you."

Emily moves to me, putting her cold hands around my neck. "Give the book over," she commands.

"If you destroy her, you destroy me," Heathcliff says, looking at me. "She is my soul and I cannot live without my soul."

He tosses *Wuthering Heights* into the fire. Coach H lunges forward, but he's too late. Emily cries out, letting go of me and grasping helplessly for the book. But as she becomes translucent to avoid the fire flames, she can't pick up the book. Her hands go through it. As we watch the flames take hold of the book, she slowly starts to disappear.

Coach H drops his head sadly.

Behind them, Ms. W and Charlotte send Mrs. Rochester back to *Jane Eyre.* Seeing her sister's book burning, Charlotte shouts and desperately tries to save the book from the fire, but it's too late. The book's pages have crumpled and turned black and Emily is fading away, bit by bit.

Alarmed, I look at Heathcliff. I expect to see him fade away, as well, but when I turn to look for him, he's gone. Disappeared. Did he disappear instantly?

I look back to Emily and see that she, too, has faded to nothingness. I sink down to my knees. He destroyed himself for me, I think, and I didn't even get a chance to thank him.

I watch the last letters on the spine of *Wuthering Heights* dissolve in blackened ash.

Ms. W comes up behind me and puts a hand on my shoulder.

"Um, guys? Can somebody untie us?" Samir asks.

"Yeah—hello—my arms are numb," Hana says.

"Does this mean we aren't going to have the apocalypse?" Blade asks, sounding disappointed.

Thirty

Among the faculty, the general consensus is that there's no way Heathcliff could've survived the burning of *Wuthering Heights* and that it was only a matter of time before he'd simply fade into oblivion. Without the book to hold him in this world, he'd be adrift, without form or powers to hurt anyone.

"But Emily said he was trapped here," I say to Charlotte, but she waves her hand.

"It's impossible," she says. "It cannot be. No character can survive without his creator. No character has ever outlasted its prose."

"And why didn't you tell me? About my ancestors?" I ask, feeling more than a little manipulated.

"We didn't know how you would take it," Ms. W says gently. "It's not an easy thing to hear."

"And face it, you probably wouldn't have believed us," Coach H says. "Next thing, you'd be asking if your grandfather is Mickey Mouse."

"We were only trying to protect you," Charlotte says.

Hana, Samir, Blade, and I return to our dorms and eventually to our classes. Things manage to go back to normal. There are no more fictional character sightings and after a month goes by without any sign of Heathcliff, I am beginning to believe that Charlotte was right: he's faded into oblivion.

This makes me very sad, because despite that everyone else thought of him as a bad guy—including Samir, Hana, and Blade, who were kidnapped by him—he did do the right thing in the end. In short, he gave his life for mine, and for that I'll always be grateful.

I try to talk to Ryan Kent, but he's still giving me the cold shoulder. And after another week, I hear he's dating Parker Rodham. Or at least she was spotted wearing his varsity basketball jacket from our old high school, which is the equivalent of a public declaration of going together. But it's my fault, really. I'm the one who blew it. Ryan goes out on a date with me and nearly dies and then I pretty much blow him off in favor of chasing after Heathcliff. I mean, he's got to think I'm not that into him.

I write Ryan a letter, apologizing, but I don't have enough guts to actually give it to him, so I give it to Samir to give to him—that is, once Samir starts talking to me again for nearly getting him killed. I also write a long letter to Dad telling him how disappointed I am in him and his neglect. I do feel better about the whole situation once I'm done. I realize that facing down death has given me a new perspective on life. This school has definitely changed me.

If I stay on here, I realize, there's a good chance I might land a scholarship. It's a lot better than my old school and I've made friends here (Hana, Samir, and even Blade) that I have to admit are a better influence than Liz and Cass. There aren't any keggers here, and no temptations to sneak out or go joyriding. There aren't any distractions. I can get serious about studying and I realize that I *like* being serious about studying. At least I know that if I work hard, I'm going to get somewhere. And let's face it, having Virginia Woolf for a teacher can only improve my chances of getting into the college of my choice.

By Thanksgiving, I've gotten the results of midterms back and I've managed to make three As and two Bs, my best report card since third grade. Things are definitely looking up.

Because of my good grades and extra credit for helping to save the school, Ms. W gives me the all clear to go home for Thanksgiving.

Mom and Lindsay pick me up from the airport, holding up a big sign that says WELCOME HOME, MIRANDA. Just seeing them again makes me get more choked up than Mom gets during an episode of the *Gilmore Girls*. I knew I missed them, but I didn't know how much. In fact, instead of avoiding Mom's menopausal hug, I run right into her arms and give her the biggest, longest squeeze of my entire life. It's Mom that tries to pull back first.

"Oh my . . . Miranda!" she exclaims, when I won't let her go. Lindsay, to her left, makes a weird face at me, so I just grab her and pull her into the bear hug. I swear, I never want to let them go.

I suppose a near-death experience with supernatural forces makes a person sentimental.

My room is (almost) as I've left it, except that Lindsay has cleaned out the remaining clothes in my closet (the thief!), but I remain calm and don't even raise my voice when I find out she's taken my softest pair of pajamas and used it to line the cage of her hamster, Fred.

"Fred missed you, I guess" is how Lindsay puts it. Which in some ways I take to mean that *she* missed me, which is sweet, I guess, except that my Paul Frank pajama bottoms are now covered in hamster poop.

I also discover that Lindsay doesn't seem to mind Mom's menopause hugs and, furthermore, that she actually *likes* hanging out with Mom and watching TV. I mean, this is how sad things are. Lindsay doesn't have any friends and she's fine with Mom being her best friend. But still, I have to admit it's nice sitting on the couch and eating pizza and listening to Mom talk about what the cast of *Everwood* is wearing. But this is okay. At this point, I'm glad even for the simple things. This includes Mom's running commentary.

It occurs to me suddenly that Mom hasn't mentioned Dad since I got home. "When do I get to see Dad?" I ask.

Lindsay looks at Mom and Mom looks back at Lindsay. Mom's Botox is wearing off so she makes a worried face, which creases a line in her forehead between her eyebrows.

"Your father and Carmen are in Tahiti," Mom says. "They're spending the holidays there and won't be back until next week."

"But I go back to school on Sunday!" I cry, unable to contain my disappointment. I can't believe Dad is letting me down—again.

"I know, honey, and I am so sorry," Mom says. "They say they're trying to work on their marriage or some such nonsense. Can you believe it? I mean, I *told* him his daughter was coming home, but did he care? No, he didn't. This is the problem with your father . . ."

I have inadvertently sent Mom on a Deadbeat Dad Diatribe, which means that for the next solid hour we're going to hear about what a jerk Dad is and how he doesn't care for us, and how he cares only for himself. Ugh. I shouldn't have asked!

Lindsay gives me a dirty look. She's probably heard this speech a million times and now she has to hear it a million more times. Well, I'm not going to feel too guilty. Lindsay didn't spend three months on Shipwreck Island eating gruel and fighting ghosts, okay? I think I definitely have had it worse.

The next day, I wake up to the smell of burning pumpkin bread, which is Mom's signature dish on Thanksgiving. When I wander into the kitchen, Lindsay is helping Mom "cook" (which in Mom's case means opening up all the prepackaged dishes from Whole Foods).

The doorbell rings and I jump a little, wondering if maybe Dad decided to make an appearance after all. It *is* Thanksgiving.

"Miranda!" shouts Lindsay from the door. "It's a *boy* and he says he's here for *you*."

I'm embarrassed already, but I'm triply embarrassed when I get to the door and I see Ryan Kent standing there.

"Miranda? Miranda, who is it?" Mom calls.

Lindsay shouts back to Mom that it's a boy and starts making kissing sounds and before I nearly die of embarrassment, I step outside and close the door, even though I don't have my coat on and it's freezing out.

"Hey," Ryan says, smiling at me.

"Hey," I say. "Sorry about that. It's my little sister. She's, well, got the mental maturity of a toddler."

"No apology necessary. I have a younger brother, Jacob. I *completely* understand."

I smile at Ryan and he smiles back, and even though a few early snow flurries start to fall around us, I feel all warm inside. This is the power of Ryan Kent. Forget cold fusion. Ryan Kent can be the world's next renewable energy source.

"How did you know where I live?" I ask him, amazed that he's found me.

"I asked around," Ryan says. "I was, uh, in the neighborhood, sort of. I wanted to stop by to tell you I got your note. Actually, I *just* got it."

"What? Samir was supposed to give that to you weeks ago," I say, suddenly thinking of the many ways I'm going to kill him. He told me he delivered it the day I gave it to him. That was more than a month ago.

"Actually, it's not Samir's fault," Ryan says. "It's my roommate. He's a total loser, and he just stuck it in a drawer and forgot to tell me it was there."

"Oh," I say. Samir just got a reprieve from a very painful death.

"I thought you and that guy Heathcliff were dating. What I saw, and what Parker said . . . well, anyway, after I got your note, I realized I was wrong," Ryan says. "I'm really sorry that I ignored you. I just felt, well, a little rejected."

"I am so sorry," I say.

"Me, too," he says. "Do you think we can start over?"

"Absolutely," I say, and then suddenly think about Parker. "That is, if Parker doesn't mind."

"Parker?" he asks, not understanding.

"Parker Rodham? Your girlfriend?"

"Oh, no, no, no. She's not my girlfriend," Ryan says. "I let her borrow my jacket once, but it was purely platonic. She likes me, I know, but the feeling isn't mutual."

My heart skips a little beat. He *never* liked Parker!

"So what are all these questions about Parker? You jealous?" he asks, teasing me a little.

"What are all these questions about Heathcliff? Are *you* jealous?"

"Yes—isn't it obvious?" he asks me, leaning in a little closer.

"No," I say, leaning in closer to him.

"Well, maybe this will prove it to you," he says, and then he puts his hands on my face, guiding it straight to his. Before I know it, his lips are on mine.

That's right.

He is *kissing* me. *On the lips.*

And it is nothing at all like Tyler's drunken, slobbery kiss or Gregory Mason's lizardlike tongue.

It's nice and warm and soft and pretty much perfect.

And all I can think is: Ryan Kent is kissing me. He's kissing me! What do I do? Okay, I stared down Emily Brontë, but when it comes to kissing, I'm lost. I'm trying to recall that ever-important "Top Things You Should Know About Kissing" *YM* article I once read, but none of the things come to mind. It doesn't matter, because my body just seems to sort of know what to do. At least, it's pretty good at winging it. My lips respond to his. Slowly, and after a long, sweet while, he draws back.

"That was really nice," he says, his big brown eyes fixed on mine.

"Y-y-yeah," I stutter, because I am well under the Influence of Ryan, which equals about four shots of Ever-clear and Red Bull.

"I wasn't sure you liked me," he says.

As if this is even possible. He wasn't sure? I've been praying for this moment since I first laid eyes on him, and he wasn't sure?

"And now?" I ask him.

"You definitely like me," he says. He smiles and puts his forehead against mine, gently resting his hand on the back of my neck, which makes my whole body shiver. I'm convinced that there's a good possibility I might not be able to form complete sentences again in my life.

"If you don't have a boyfriend," Ryan says, "are you taking auditions for one?"

"Er . . ." I stutter. Because I am so articulate at times like these.

"Well, how was that? For my audition?"

"You are definitely in the top five finalists," I manage to joke.

"Well, if I am boyfriend material, I'd like to give you this," he says, handing me a shiny red bag.

"But I didn't get you anything," I say.

"Don't worry. It's not something I bought," he says, smiling at me.

I pull out his old basketball letterman's jacket from our old high school.

"Does this mean what I think it means?" I ask him.

"Would you, uh, you know . . ." He pauses and

shifts his weight from foot to foot, clearly uncomfortable. ". . . wear it?"

Is he kidding? I'm going to sleep in it.

"Yes! Yes, of course!" I put it on now, in fact, and then I throw my arms around his neck and give him a kiss. It's only about two seconds before the porch light starts flickering on and off. I see Lindsay through the window by the door. She's the one behind the light show. God, how embarrassing. Mom is also there. She taps on the window, a look of disapproval on her face.

"Uh, I guess I should go," Ryan says, "But maybe we could grab a movie or something? You know, before we have to go back."

"Yes, definitely. And maybe even more Pop-Tarts?"

Ryan's smile gets bigger. "Absolutely," he says.

I watch him as he walks back to his car. I was already kind of looking forward to going back to Bard, as crazy as that sounds—and now here's another reason. Ryan Kent. Dad, after all, paid for a full year of tuition, with no refunds. I'm in for *at least* a year at Bard, so I might as well get used to it.

A UPS truck pulls up just as Ryan jumps into his car (his mom's sedan) and drives off. The delivery guy hops out in front of our house and brings up a package. It's wrapped in brown paper and tied with a white string.

"Miranda Tate?" he asks.

I nod and he hands the package over to me.

I walk inside the house, to the curious stares of Mom

and Lindsay, wearing Ryan's letterman jacket and holding the UPS package.

"If it's from Dad, it's mine! Mine!" Lindsay cries, taking the package out of my hand and ripping it open. "What's this?" Lindsay says, holding up a round locket on a gold chain.

"It's mine; give it back," I snap, taking it out of her hands. It's a gold locket and inside there's a tiny scrap of paper folded over. I take it out and unfold it. It looks like . . . a piece of a page of *Wuthering Heights*. It's slightly charred, but the letters are distinct on the page. The only word I see intact is: "Heathcliff."

Is it possible? Does he live?

With the locket, there's a note in shaky handwriting.

It says, "Cathy lives in you, and so does my soul. So long as you exist, so do I. Yours forever, H."

Heathcliff? Did he save this bit of the book somehow? Does he live still?

And where did he learn to write?

I grab the package wrappings off the floor and see the sent date. It was the day before yesterday. Heathcliff is alive! Here's definitive proof.

"Who's H?" Lindsay asks, looking over my shoulder.

"No one," I say.

I fold up the piece of paper, put it in the necklace, and put the necklace around my neck. He's given me his life—literally. This scrap of paper means he's still connected to this world. I wonder if this means Emily Brontë is, too?

"That better not be from that boy—what's his name—Tyler," Mom says, looking stern. As if I'd have anything to do with Tyler ever again. Please. "And just *who* was that boy outside? You know my rules about dating, Miranda."

"Uh-oh, Miranda's in trouble again," Lindsay says. "She's going back to Bard!"

"I'm going back anyway, you nitwit," I say. "Dad prepaid for the year and there aren't any refunds."

"Miranda, you know the rules," Mom says, eyeing the locket and the letterman jacket I'm wearing. "No dates until you're sixteen. And no boyfriends, either."

I'm not quite sure how to tell Mom, but it looks like I don't just have one boyfriend. I have two.

And I know one thing for sure. This is going to mean trouble in more ways than one when I get back to Bard next semester.

Big trouble.

Your attitude. Your style.
MTV Books:
Totally your type.

Cruel Summer

First in the
Fast Girls, Hot Boys
series!

Kylie Adams

Life is a popularity contest...and someone is about to lose. In sexy Miami Beach, five friends are wrapping up high school—but one of them won't make it to graduation alive....

The Pursuit of Happiness
Tara Altebrando

Declare your independence....After her mother dies and her boyfriend cheats on her, Betsy picks up the pieces of her devastated life and finds remarkable strength and unexpected passion.

Life as a Poser
First in
the *310*
series!

Beth Killian

Sometimes you have to fake it to make it....Eva spends an intoxicating summer in glamorous Hollywood with her famous talent agent aunt in this witty, pop culture-savvy novel, first in a new series.

Plan B
Jenny O'Connell

Plan A didn't know about him....When her movie-star half brother—a total teen heartthrob—comes to town, one very practical girl's plans for graduation and beyond are blown out of the water.

Available wherever books are sold.

Published by Pocket Books
A Division of Simon & Schuster
A CBS Company

www.simonsays.com/mtvbooks

14330

As many as 1 in 3 Americans
have HIV and don't know it.

TAKE CONTROL.
KNOW YOUR STATUS.
GET TESTED.

To learn more about HIV testing,
or get a free guide to HIV and
other sexually transmitted diseases.

www.knowhivaids.org
1-866-344-KNOW